Quayse grew up Peterborough Ontario, the second of five children. She has always loved reading and writing and working with children. Another passion is needle work, particularly embroidery for pillows.

For family, conversation, and education

Quayse Hurlington

MY KNIGHT IN RUSTY ARMOR

AUSTIN MACAULEY PUBLISHERS™
LONDON • CAMBRIDGE • NEW YORK • SHARJAH

Copyright © Quayse Hurlington 2023

All rights reserved. No part of this publication may be reproduced, distributed, or transmitted in any form or by any means, including photocopying, recording, or other electronic or mechanical methods, without the prior written permission of the publisher, except in the case of brief quotations embodied in critical reviews and certain other noncommercial uses permitted by copyright law. For permission requests, write to the publisher.

Any person who commits any unauthorized act in relation to this publication may be liable to criminal prosecution and civil claims for damages.

This is a work of fiction. Names, characters, businesses, places, events, locales, and incidents are either the products of the author's imagination or used in a fictitious manner. Any resemblance to actual persons, living or dead, or actual events is purely coincidental.

Ordering Information:
Quantity sales: special discounts are available on quantity purchases by corporations, associations, and others. For details, contact the publisher at the address below.

Publisher's Cataloging-in-Publication data
Hurlington, Quayse
My Knight in Rusty Armor

ISBN 9781645363422 (Paperback)
ISBN 9781645362197 (Hardback)
ISBN 9781645365211 (ePub e-book)

Library of Congress Control Number: 2023902311

www.austinmacauley.com/us

First Published 2023
Austin Macauley Publishers LLC
40 Wall Street, 33rd Floor, Suite 3302
New York, NY 10005
USA

mail-usa@austinmacauley.com
+1 (646) 5125767

I'd like to begin by acknowledging my church family who have so much room to grow and learn.

Table of Contents

Prologue

"He did what!"

Essie glanced side to side and bowed her head to hide blushing cheeks from her friend. "Kate, keep it down!"

"Why? It's a relationship, not a secret," Kate twirled a clump of berry-blond hair around a finger and dipped her head toward Essie's, mimicking her pose. "So... has he kissed you?"

Essie blushed.

"He hasn't! What! You've been on what... 3? 4 dates? And he asked you to be his *girlfriend!*—and he hasn't kissed you yet?"

"Katie Troy. Hush!" Essie pleaded.

"Esmeralda Ann... whatever the rest of your name is— Landry!" Kate glared.

Essie ignored her and kept talking, "So he took me to church and introduced me to his friends and then the pastor asked who I was, and he said, 'my future wife!' That's a quote!" Essie giggled.

"Ess," Kate grabbed her friend's hand and met her eyes, suddenly serious, "You're not actually going to *marry* that boy, are you?"

Essie's sage-colored eyes darkened as she took on a look, dreamy and soft. "I don't know, Katie."

"You want to!" Kate said accusingly.

"I hardly know him," Essie brushed her off and tucked some blond hair back behind her ear.

Later that night, alone in her apartment, goodnight texts were sent, and blankets were pulled up to her chin, Esmeralda smiled to herself, remembering him. The touch of his hand on hers when he offered her the hymnbook or collection plate. His dark hair that she had to hold herself back from brushing away from his brown eyes.

Everyone talked about brown eyes as if they're boring. His weren't. They were the color of the earth after rain. They're hazelnuts and gingerbread men and chocolate brownies, and they're the feeling of coming inside from the biting cold and being wrapped in the softest of blankets by the person you love. They're cocoa and coffee and tea. They're cinnamon and ginger and cassia, and they're the dust from horse hooves, pulling a romantic carriage. They're the soft, imagined warmness of his hand on her waist.

Essie rolled over and curled up in a fetal position on her bed. She wrapped her arms around herself and closed her eyes. She fell asleep with a smile on her face.

Months Later

"You're really going to marry this guy!" Kate collapsed into a heap of blue taffeta mournfully.

"I mean, I like him—I guess—but I didn't..."

"You could be a little happy for her, Katelyn," Kyra Landry admonished.

"Mom, be nice," Essie turned her head.

"Esmeralda!" Kyra exclaimed.

"Sorry, Mama," Essie looked straight again, and her mom continued fixing her veil. "But, Kate, please! Get up. You'll wrinkle your dress. This is really important to me!" Essie pleaded.

Kate stood accordingly and pecked Ms. Landry on the cheek. "I am happy for her, Mama K. But I don't want her to grow up. She's acting like a grown-up."

"As she should be. Good thing that the bridesmaid dress is blue, my dear. Green is an ugly color on you," Kyra tried to look sternly at Kate but couldn't manage and folded her into her arms.

"Katie, you could be getting married too. You've been with that Alec boy for how long? He's a good boy... and from the church too."

Kate made a face behind Kyra's back. "Sorry, Mama K. I don't think I'm the marrying type."

"Every woman is the marrying type. Remember, a virtuous woman, worth more than rubies; she brings her husband good, and her children arise and call her blessed; her husband also, and he praises her. That's Proverbs 31 and another verse…"

"Mama," Essie called, acknowledging Kate's relief at the sparing of a lecture. "It's almost time for you to go get ready with Mama Amy."

"Can I dissuade you from calling her that?" Kyra said softly and took Essie's hands. "I know, I know 'A man and a woman should leave their father's household and cleave to each other' but I'm losing my only baby girl," she gathered Essie's in her arms.

"You'll never stop being my mommy, but now I'll have another one too," Essie answered, squeezing her mom in return. "His mom is my mom now, and you're his mama too."

"You'll finally have a daddy too," Kyra pointed out. "I wish my Max could be here with us today. He'd be so proud of you, all grown-up and glad that you found your Mr. Darcy," Kyra kissed Essie's head.

"Mama, you'll be late," Essie pushed her toward the door, gently.

"I know, Esmeralda. I'm going! I'm going," she kissed Essie one more time and left the little room at the back of the church.

"Finally," Essie sighed.

"How are you feeling, honey?" Kate picked up a folded bit of paper to start fanning her. "You know it's not too late to…"

"No, I'm going through with this," Essie laughed. "You just stop that, Miss Katelyn," she spread her white gown all around her carefully and lowered herself to the floor. She propped her chin up on one hand and smiled a little. "I feel… I feel like I want to collapse and cry for hours from the stress, but then I think about him. And I think that after this I'll be with him forever. And then I want to just run down the aisle into his arms."

"You'd better not, Miss Esmeralda Landry," Kate warned. "You've spent months planning this wedding. You'd better not go and mess it all up."

"Kate, it's about the marriage, not the wedding," Essie went on in her dreamy tone.

Kate sank to her knees beside her friend and then lay on her back, head on Essie's lap, staring up at the ceiling. "You know that 50% of marriages break up, right? How can you make yourself go through this anyway?"

"Kate, that's about the most dismal and rude thing you could say to a bride on her wedding day!" Essie burst out laughing.

"But really, Ess," Kate insisted. "How can you go through with it, knowing that it won't work out?"

"That's where you're wrong," Essie smiled serenely. She ran a hand over Kate's perfectly brushed and twisted-up red hair. "We'll be the 50% that make it."

"Don't you bet that every couple thinks that? I mean, no one is like, 'hey, we should get married. I bet we'll end up getting divorced! Let's do it!' No one thinks that."

"We did everything right, though," Essie insisted, closing her eyes happily. "We're both from the church; we did Bible studies together and went to church together. We met each other's families. We never so much as kissed while we courted; he was a perfect gentleman; and I was a lady. Even our wedding will be proper," she stood and dumped Kate off of her lap to spin around.

"My dress is the one that my mom wore when she was married, only remodeled for the weather—she was married in winter you know—it's white for purity. You, my best friend in the whole world, are the maid of honor. The colors are white, blue, and gold. White for purity, blue for loyalty and fidelity, gold for a prosperous life."

"Is that really the way to have a good marriage? You guys had a sort of old-fashioned courtship. I mean, not kissing! I've kissed 8 guys, and I was only dating two of them," Kate exclaimed.

"Not everyone has what we have. Not everyone wants it either," Essie shrugged.

"Ess, what's it feel like?" Kate demanded getting up and grabbing her friend's arm, with a face full of honest curiosity and even a little jealousy. "Having been that chaste. Do you even desire him? If you did, there's no way that you could have controlled yourselves this long! And now you'll be sharing your first kiss in front of everyone…"

"It… it feels right. I love that I am so pure for him. That he'll be my first for everything. I feel like it means I can be completely his since I've never been with anyone else."

"Oh, my *lord*, Esmeralda!" Kate grabbed her shoulders. "Stop calling him *Him*, like he *is* God. He has a name!"

Essie gave that perfectly calm and peaceful smile that made her entire face lit up. "Eli. Elias Michael Darcy!"

"A real Mr. Darcy," Kate remarked dryly. "And my stupid cousin. I never would have introduced you if I had known you'd fall in love!"

Essie broke into carefree laughter. She hugged herself around the waist and spun across the room giggling, "Katie! I'm so in love. I can't *stand* it!"

The pastor puts his hand on Eli's shoulder, pulling him back to reality. "Son, it's almost time to go out."

Elias jumped a little bit and shook his head free of the beautiful daydream. He smiled guiltily at the pastor. "Okay. Tell me when," he waited for the man to walk away and leave him with his dreams, but he stayed there. "Anything else?" Eli asked.

Pastor James smiled knowingly. "Are you keeping your thoughts pure, Son?"

Eli looked at the ground. "I… uh… I'm eager for her to be my wife, pastor."

"I'm sure you are. God created the act of lovemaking. It is perfectly natural for you to desire your bride that way."

Eli blushed beet red and started a few sentences, unable to finish any of them. Pastor James's face lit up in laughter. "I remember when you first introduced that young woman to me. She's really quite remarkable, isn't she?"

"Yes, Sir," Eli said wistfully.

"She'll be a good wife to you."

"I always knew she would be."

"Too good for you, likely!" another voice called over those of the pastor and Eli. Another young man sauntered over and grinned a freckled face at Elias.

Pastor James smiled at him and quoted, "Thou shalt not covet thy neighbor's wife…" before walking away laughing. "I'll see you two upfront in ten minutes."

"Andy," Eli rolled his eyes.

Andrew gave a perfect twirl. "What do you think? This is a good color for me."

"Yeah, Esmeralda picked it," Eli rolled his eyes again. "But I don't think she did so with your preferences in mind."

"Probably not," Andy grinned, "but I look so dapper in it that even at the altar, she might *finally* fall in love with me and kiss your ass goodbye."

"I doubt it," Eli said, bristling.

Andy noticed and threw an arm around Elias in concern. "Hey, I'm kidding. That girl is loyal to the core. And she loves you. Besides, she and Kate have been best friends for years, which means that as Kate's big brother, I had to annoy her for years. So many years that if she liked me like that, we would already be married."

"I'm not worried," Eli shrugged.

Andy ignored him and folded him into a bear hug. "Aww shi… ah… shivareeing! Course, you are. I can't believe you're getting married. And to Essie! My little sister's best friend. I can't believe she's marrying you, you knucklehead! I mean, my roguish good looks against your whatever. And my impeccable family…"

"We have the same grandparents, lil cousin," Eli retorted.

"Oh, yeah. Small details," Andy grinned.

They stood in silence for another few moments before Andy said, "Are you actually nervous?"

"A little. Not much. I know that this is God's plan for my life. Is to be with Esmeralda."

Andy smiled with only a little smile. "You love her, huh."

"So, so much," Eli said earnestly. "You can't possibly understand it."

"I guess not," Andy shrugged. "Hey, there's Pastor James. It's time to go in," he gripped Eli's arm. "Come on."

"Wait. Can we pray first?" Eli asked, blushing a bit but standing his ground.

"For what! You're already as blessed as possible. We'll be late," Andy tugged him forward.

"No, I really need to. I want God involved in every aspect of our relationship," Eli pressed.

"I know when I'm beaten. You know, you're so much of a better person than I," Andy shook his head. He reached for Eli's hands, and they bowed their heads together.

Andy grinned and extended an arm. "Milady sister," he bowed. Kate scowled and took it as lightly as possible. From the front of the church, besides Pastor James, Eli saw his cousins and best friends walk perfectly in sync together to the front of the church and split off to the sides.

The music suddenly changed, and all of Eli's view was taken up by the stunning little figure in white, elegant, and composed and his. All his.

Chapter 1

Essie woke up slowly. She was warm all over, having created a little pocket of heat, curled up with her new husband under the down comforter they had picked out together. She stirred and suddenly felt him there. Hard chest pressed against tender breasts. One of his arms was thrown over her waist while the other was tucked under his head. She felt the rise and fall of his heart. His heart, that's all hers.

Then she opened her eyes. Her heart fluttered as she took in the flawless skin and tender expression on his sleeping face. His eyelashes brushing over perfect cheeks. The tiny stubble on his chin and jawbone.

So much love and adoration washed over her followed by a rivulet of fear. She shouldn't be here. She shouldn't be in bed with a man! It went against everything she was taught as a girl growing up in a church and with her single mom. "flee from sexual immorality" and all that. She felt guilt well up in her stomach as if she ate some bad meat. She started to pull away when she caught a flash of gold on her hand.

She stopped and stared at her wedding ring. She looked back down at the man lying next to her. The cold air prickled her naked body, and she looked with longing at his warm, supplicating body. Her husband. Eli Darcy. He murmured in his sleep and pulled her closer to him. Her husband. That meant that she could be in bed with him, right? Essie sighed happily and slipped back under the blankets. Intertwining her legs with his to get as close to him as possible. His arm tightened around her waist, and she nestled against him. Her breath mingling with his as she drifted off back to sleep; their two hearts thumping together.

When Essie woke up a second time, it's by a gentle mouth coaxing her closer. She sighed happily and kissed him back. The dark head leaning over her shyly kissed a trail from her lips to her neck, down over one shoulder, down toward a rounded chest, waking her skin to his touch. Suddenly shy, Essie shrank back from his caresses.

Without needing to say anything, Eli tipped her chin up to him, gently, and kissed her mouth. He grazed his lips over hers, and when she responded positively, only then did he increase the passion of the embrace. He held her tight and slipped one hand through the sea of golden curls spilling over the white pillowcases.

"Good morning, wife," Eli said. His voice was rough from just waking up. He brushed a thumb over her rosy cheeks and relaxed back onto the pillows, drawing Essie to lie on his chest.

"Good morning, husband," Essie blushed all pink. She wondered if he could tell how she felt this morning, how disorienting it was to wake up away from home in someplace that was supposed to be her new home. She wondered if he could tell last night and this morning how strange it was to be so free and liberal with affection and how strange and frightening it was to let him touch her like that after 22 years of being so careful not to let anyone touch her so carnally. She wondered if he felt any of those feelings himself. She felt so young and vulnerable, even against the comforting solidity of her beloved's body.

"I love you, Mrs. Esmeralda Darcy," Elias said suddenly. "I've wanted to call you that for so long. I've wanted to wake up like this with you for so long. Since Kate first introduced us."

Essie blushed at the mention of her friend. Kate had no place in this perfect marital room. It's all theirs. Their bedroom where their love was made corporeal. She guessed Eli felt no shame or guilt at all.

"You're so quiet, Esmeralda," Elias broke the perfect silence again. "Not like the Essie I know. Did Mama K pull Rachel and Leah on me? Let me look at you and see for sure that you are the bride I wanted."

He pulled the blankets off of her a bit more and looks longingly, adoringly over her body. Essie flushed. She felt loved and embarrassed all at once. She burrowed under the quilt and squealed when Eli's hand squeezed her thigh unexpectedly. "Elias!" she said reproachfully, cheeks as hot as fire.

"There she is," he laughed.

A breeze ruffled the organza curtains, partially opened to let in the fresh air. Essie remembered picking out those curtains. Thinking about the first time she would wake up in this bed with this man and look out at the billowy pale-green drapes. She didn't think it would be like this. This… awkward!

"So what now?" Essie blurted, reddening.

"Now? Whatever we want!" Elias exclaimed. He picked her up and swung her into his lap, kissing her soundly. "Whatever we want, gem! We're married and young and in love!"

Essie giggled, despite herself and maybe even because of it.

"Remember why we chose not to go on a traditional honeymoon? We wanted to just start married life together. Want to make me breakfast?" Eli grinned.

"No," Essie retorted.

"My Esmeralda," Eli hugged her tight around the waist. "We could stay in bed all day…" Eli suggested.

"Okay."

"Okay?"

"Okay. I could use some more sleep."

"Beds aren't for sleeping, gem," Eli leaned forward and touched her nose with his. "They're for making babies."

Essie quickly crossed herself.

"What are you doing! You're not even Catholic!"

"No, but I'm taking every measure possible other than birth control to ask God to have an intervention with your sperm and my eggs. I hope to God we didn't make a baby last night," Essie shuddered.

Eli furrowed his forehead. "I thought you wanted kids."

"Well, yeah, one or two and not right away," Essie insisted. "I don't want to share you," she murmured shyly.

"I didn't know you had a jealous streak," Eli grinned. He didn't know why he kept pressing the issue. He kept teasing her and poking her in a way he never would have done before they were married. He guessed it's because he didn't want to scare her away. But now she's his! His wife.

Essie changed the subject, stretching lazily. "I feel like I should get up and do something productive, but I really don't want to move."

Eli's mouth went a little bit dry as he saw her pert little breasts rise ever so slightly above the comforter. One time, near the end of their engagement period, she had worn a low-cut shirt that showed the slightest bit of cleavage. He had to stop himself from touching her then. Literally, hold himself back. Now, he had full rights over her body and she over his, and still, he hesitated. Eli had felt her freeze and shrank back earlier. He didn't want to scare her by acting like some kind of animal in heat. He didn't want her to know how much he desired her. He reminded himself that this was a virtuous woman who had guarded her virginity with force for 22 years, and of course, it would be difficult to be comfortable with her body and him right away. But now, as defensive as she had seemed earlier, Esmeralda was looking up at him with adoring, yielding big eyes.

Essie peeped up toward Eli through her eyelashes. She suddenly missed his touch on her awakened bare skin. She stretched a little bit, showing more skin above the covers, and saw him follow the curve of her bosom and waist all the way to the end. But he didn't touch her. Essie felt her heart do a funny twist and felt ashamed. He didn't want her right now. Should she be ashamed at having pushed herself at him? Would he be upset if she made the first move? She couldn't make herself do it, and so they simply lay there for a moment.

"Elias…" Essie began, "I…" she didn't know what to say or what to do. She felt less like a newlywed to a man she loved and more like a little girl acting a part too grown-up for her. She hung her head as her cheeks go bright red, and the flush was mimicked all down her body.

Eli looked down at the blushing bride he had carried over the threshold 15 hours ago. Still, she was blushing, but she was quiet, nervous seeming. Eli's heart melted. He could see that she wanted to say something and couldn't find the words. He was struck by her youth. Her beautiful body and spirit in the prime of her youth. "Everything okay, Esmeralda?"

She looked back up at him finally and half nodded. She took on a stern expression, and as if before she could change her mind about something, she reached over and put a hand on his chest.

Eli was still letting her do what she wanted. He suddenly felt stupid. She had wanted him to touch her earlier. That's what all the stretching and looks were about. She didn't know how to tell him. Poor girl, she needed him to take control. But for this moment, she needed to take control on her own and discover what she was capable of. Eli gasped a breath as her little fingers moved over him. He had doubts that she had any idea what she was capable of.

Essie felt Eli shudder underneath her and felt a surge of pride. She did that. She made him do that. She hesitated for another moment, unsure where to go from there. Her eyes met his, and he grinned. "I love you, Esmeralda."

"I love you too, Elias."

He had her on her back quickly, doing things to her that she thought might be forbidden by the church but couldn't care less.

Every day of that week, Eli woke Essie with passionate kisses and loving words and teased her skin awake until she responded to him after only seconds. They went out for dinner every night, and Essie reveled in the joy and pride of having a husband. It was like having won a prize. She figured. She had won Elias. The perfect handsome man that she could claim as her own.

Then one night, Eli took much more care and time making love to her. Having finished, he kissed her sweetly. "Esmeralda…" he sighed against her mouth. She kissed him back, resting her blond head against his chest. He weaved his legs around hers, pressing himself to her. She could feel his silent question but didn't answer.

Eli shrugged a little to himself. He knew he wouldn't get another round; it was worth a shot anyway. It didn't bother him much that his pretty little wife wasn't as passionate as he. He chalked it up to male hormones and wasn't offended when she rolled over, curling up to him spoon style. But Eli had a special reason for wanting her so badly tonight.

"Tomorrow, we have to go back to life. You have to finish school, and I have to go back to work," Elias murmured into the darkness.

"Do I have to?" Essie whispered back. "I just want to stay home with you."

"I promised your Ma that you'd finish your program. The only way she'd let us get married this early, remember?" Elias stroked her curly head and burrowed his face into the soft patch of skin between her neck and shoulder. "Only 6 more months, gem."

"Eli…"

"Esmeralda," he whined back. "What would I tell Mama K?"

Essie fell quiet. She found it hard to believe that being with Eli as a wife was so different than being with him as a girlfriend. She couldn't bear to leave his side. And she was suddenly fiercely jealous at the thought of him at work with other women.

"What are you thinking about, gem?"

"Umm…" Essie thought hard.

"Be honest, Esmeralda."

"I was thinking about you with other girls," Essie admitted.

"Esmeralda Darcy!" Eli exclaimed, propping himself up on one arm. "What a thought!"

"I'm sorry."

"I wouldn't ever!"

"I know."

"Never ever! Honestly, I never saw you as the jealous type."

"I know! And thank goodness!" Essie snipped. "You're mine," she turned back to face him and then, after a brief hesitation, straddled him, moving with delicious friction.

Eli grinned and closed his eyes in delight. If he had known that it would be so easy to get her in the mood, he would have done it earlier.

Chapter 2

Essie woke up early, determined to do something nice for Eli before she had to leave for the day. She had to tear herself out of his warm arms, but she managed. She showered alone and got dressed.

In the quiet hours of the morning, Essie padded through the house alone. She remembered buying the house as she went through. They had been so organized. Saving for two years prior to even their engagement. Essie had known he was the one. Essie trailed a hand over the back of the sofa and then a chair. She touched the framed picture of their wedding that was the only thing on the shelf. They had wanted to start fresh together. She wandered into the kitchen and touched the curtains. They're the same ones as were in the bedroom. Light green and tied back with red ribbons.

She tied them back to watch the sunrise as she cooked. She slipped a Mother Hubbard over her blouse, not because she's afraid of sullying it, but because it made her feel so wifely.

Eli woke up alone. For a moment he didn't know where he was. He had never been alone in this bed before. He opened his eyes to see if the other side of the bed was really empty. It was but Eli, now awake and alert, felt at home even without her. When Elias wandered into the kitchen, it felt like home too but a better version. Esmeralda was there.

The sweet smells of syrup and fruit and pancakes wafted into the air. The early summer air kept the room at a good temperature. And, of course, his darling wife stood by the table, arranging a vase of flowers, honey-gold curls tumbling down her back. Eli, smiling, wrapped his arms around her waist from behind, inhaling the scent of her hair and skin.

Essie squealed in surprise, turning her head sharply and sending all that hair flying into Eli's face. He pressed a soft kiss to the side of her neck.

"Look at you, Mrs. Darcy. So pretty and… did you make me breakfast?"

Essie turned around and giggled. "I wanted to do something nice. I'll miss you all day long."

"I'll miss you too, gem."

They sat and joined hands, and Eli prayed over the meal. Essie left her head bowed for a few moments after the amen. She breathed a quick prayer that God would forgive her for being distracted by her husband, even during prayer.

All through the meal, Essie watched him adoringly. So far having a husband was like having a best friend or a boyfriend only if he could have his carnal way. He was much more interested in the sex than she, but Essie didn't mind.

Every time Eli looked up, he met Essie's eyes. A soft green-gray, yielding, and loving. He remembered when they were as bright as jewels.

Essie shook hands with her last teacher. Exuberant, she picked up the hem of her dress and skipped toward the refreshments table. Done high school! Forever! A friend touched her arm, and Essie turned around and squealed with her. Essie left the girl and picked out a cookie off of the table. She started to leave then glanced around surreptitiously before grabbing another one. Backing away, Essie suddenly crashed into another person. Mortified, she jumped away. He reached down and put a steadying hand on her shoulder. "I'm sorry. My fault."

"Not at all," Essie blushed and hurried away. It wasn't lost on her how attractive the man was but manners drilled into her for the last four years held her back from approaching him.

He felt the same pull to her but couldn't introduce himself, an older man, to a young girl at her graduation party. He knew he would find a way to speak with her, though. He couldn't get her out of his mind. Elias watched as she, with dancer-like grace, moved through the room stopping here and there to exchange handshakes and hugs.

Andy threw an arm over Eli's shoulders. "Elias… ohhhhhh, that face. Who is she?"

"Who's who?" Eli bluffed.

"I know the face. You're surrounded by beautiful young Christian girls, and you think you found wifey," Andy grinned.

Kate sidled over and took Eli's arm. Half a dozen girls around who had been looking at Eli with interest suddenly found importance elsewhere when the queen bee herself was acknowledged by the handsome stranger. "My cousin," Kate winked to the girl beside her. The news spread like fire, and suddenly, the girls were interested again. "You don't think you might be too old for these girls? Most of us are barely 18."

"It's not that much," Elias rolled his eyes. "Trust me, she's the one. Besides, she is definitely wifey. This all-girls Christian school is grooming you to be old-fashioned women and wives. Like two of all of them are going to post-secondary, and 90% of these girls are already engaged."

"So you just want a girl that will make you breakfast and look pretty on your arm at church and sew her own maternity clothes?" Kate demanded.

"No! But I want a Christian woman with all the same values and ideals as you, pretty cousin. And these girls are pure and pretty. Look, they even made all of you wear white to graduate in. The color of purity," Eli laughed, pinching an inch of Kate's skirt.

"So which one is she?" Andy laughed along.

Eli didn't even have to scan the crowd. His eye had never left the slim, beautiful blond in all white. She stood out from the crowd with elegance and maturity the other girls couldn't even get close to. "Her," he nodded toward her.

Andy burst out laughing. "Her!"

Kate punched his arm. "That's my best friend! Of everyone here, you got caught on her!"

"I would say he has impeccable taste. Want to fight me for the maiden?" Andy grinned bigger.

"Kate, introduce me? Please!" Eli begged. "I need to meet her."

"Her has a name!" Kate snapped.

"What is it?" Elias asked eagerly.

Kate rolled her eyes again. "Esmeralda."

"Ess?"

Essie turned around with a start. "Katie! Can you believe we made it through?"

"Hardly," Kate answered with a strained smile. "Hey, Ess, I have someone to introduce you to."

"Okay?"

Kate beckoned him forward, and Eli reached for her hand, bowing slightly as he shook it. "Essie, this is my idiot cousin Elias. Eli, Esmeralda."

"Oh!" Essie gasped, eyes widening. "I think we met briefly before," she blushed bright red.

"I won't count it if you don't," Eli winked.

It was a forward gesture. But friendly. Essie teetered between laughing and being shocked and decided to laugh. He had a charm about him…

"I won't count it then. It's good to meet you, Elias."

"May I take you for a walk outside?" Eli pressed.

Essie shook her head so sharply that her delicate coif should have come undone. "We would need a chaperone. School rules."

"Just like the 1800s," Eli nodded in mock seriousness.

Essie found herself laughing again. "But we could walk along the outside of the room?" she suggested.

"That would be really nice, Esmeralda."

They walked and talked. He told her about his job as a legal officer to the CEO of BlueCo, about the Christian school he had gone to for four years—the boy equivalent to this one—and that his favorite color was purple. She put away her giggles and told him that she wanted to pursue nursing and had gotten into a two-year program in the area on one of two full-ride scholarships for women. She told him about how she had met Kate and that her favorite color was green.

Then he stopped her and looked into her eyes, resisting the magnetic force that wanted him to pull her tightly to him and kiss her deeply. "Green. Like your eyes. And kind of like your name. Esmeralda is kind of like Emerald-Ella."

"That's not what my mama was thinking when she named me. She named me after the Disney princess. But since the church would definitely frown on that, we can tell them that I'm Emerald-Ella," Essie laughed.

Eli didn't move. "I've heard that emeralds are the most precious stone to set into jewelry and also the toughest next to diamonds."

"That's interesting," Essie said breathlessly.

"What about you, Emerald-Ella? Are you tough?" he asked in a low voice that made her shiver by the intimacy of the conversation.

"Tough as nails," she answered. She bowed her head to hide her blush but only for a moment before she looked up again, meeting his sure gaze as if to prove her point.

"Nay. I think tough as gems. Strong and beautiful," he touched her nose playfully to break the moment, but she still felt warm all over.

They kept walking and approached a section with a few steps upward. He paused to offer her his arm to go up. Essie looked at him in surprise and then affection. "You're just a regular gentleman, aren't you?"

Eli winked. "There's nothing common about me, gem."

"Okay, Mr. Darcy."

He blinked a few times. "How do you know my name?"

"Oh," Essie blushed. "Mr. Darcy is a book character. He's a perfect gentleman and handsome and eloquent."

"But my name really is Darcy," his eyes opened wide.

Hers followed, as bright as the emerald stones. "No way."

He bowed. "Elias Michael Darcy."

"Do you believe in fate, Mr. Darcy?" Essie peeked up at him through pale lashes.

"Nay, Miss Esmeralda. But I do believe in God."

Eli looked at the woman in front of him now and promised himself that he would plan a nice romantic evening for her tonight or at the latest tomorrow. He loved romantic gestures and besides, anything for Mrs. Darcy.

"You'll be late, my love," Elias said reluctantly.

"I know," Essie mourned. She got up and started cleaning the table off. Dishes went to the dishwasher; leftovers went to the freezer. Essie picked up the open pitcher of maple syrup and hurried to stash it in the fridge.

"Esmeralda!" Eli called in concern. "That's a terrible idea. Nothing in there is balanced well. It'll spill."

"No, it won't! Besides, I have to hurry. I'll cover it in the morning."

Elias looked dubitably at the slammed fridge, but in a rush, he grabbed his coat and keys and briefcase instead of checking it. Essie said she would deal with it. He trusted that she would.

Essie walked into her first class a few minutes late. She felt like everyone's watching her and that the shiny gold band on her hand attracted too much attention. She took a seat in the back of the lecture hall, trying not to interrupt.

She was reassured that Kate came into the class even later than she. Kate saw her in the back and hurried over, bumping into a few tables as she went, apologizing loudly. Essie would have looked away if it weren't so funny. Kate dropped her sports bag and her backpack onto the floor and dragged out a chair next to Essie's. It grated against the floor, and Essie covered her eyes against the squeal and the embarrassment.

"You're so late. Class is half over," Essie smirked.

"I had to shower after rugby practice," Kate answered. "And I bet you only just got in like five minutes before me. You're perpetually late, and you don't have an excuse."

"I had a superb excuse."

Kate didn't care. She grabbed for Essie's hand to ooh over her wedding band. She hugged her friend tight and demanded, "So what's it like being married?" Essie's face lit up, and Kate almost regretted asking. She knew she's about to get a lecture about how wonderful it was. "Lemme guess. Divine?"

Essie's eyes took on that soft quality, and she whispered, "Perfectly divine!"

"I'm not jealous," Kate huffed, slouching down in her seat.

"You sure…?" Essie teased, fluttering her ringed finger near Kate's face.

A group of students sitting around them turned to glare, and Kate lowered her voice before insisting, "Yes! I don't want to get married."

"What about Alec?"

She shrugged, "He's fun. But I wouldn't want to marry him. Especially not this young. I have a fun life to live!"

"Marriage is fun," Essie grinned. "It's like friendship but with some… bonuses."

"Gross. He's my cousin."

"Your cousin is hot."

"Essie!"

The students turned around again and made eye pointed faces at Essie and Kate. Kate mouthed sorry, and the two girls turned back to the lecturer. Essie could feel Kate's gaze on her and hid a smile as she stared straight ahead.

Kate and Essie were the first to leave the class and go for lunch. Kate kept making faces at her as they walked across campus and silently sat through another lecture. Kate glared at her as Essie went off serenely to her class, and Kate went to her respective elective. They came back together at the end of the day for their last lab. Under the pretense of working on the project, Essie was quiet.

Finally, Kate elbowed her with a ferocity that couldn't be ignored. Essie turned to her and stuck out her tongue. "What do you want?"

"How's the sex?" Kate demanded.

Essie blushed. "You sure you want to know? He's your cousin," she stalled.

"Esssss," Kate pleaded. "I've been so patient."

Essie stared down at her clipboard and made a few notes. "I guess you have. But it's none of your business you know. I don't kiss and tell."

Kate elbowed her again, "Esmeralda!"

"My name is not a weapon, Katelyn," Essie quipped.

"You know mine damn well is," Kate glared. "Tell me! Please! I need to know if I should do it with Alec."

Essie stopped cold, "You're not married to him."

"So? Most people aren't married when they start gettin' it on," Kate widened her eyes innocently.

"But you should be," Essie exclaimed. "You're not of the world. Just in it. You know what the church believes," Essie looked shocked. "You're not thinking of leaving the church, are you?"

"No, you silly. I agree with most of the church's beliefs…"

"But?"

"But I don't think God will send me to hell if I express physical love to my boyfriend."

"Kate, please don't!" Essie pleaded.

Kate pretended to think about it for a moment. "You know… maybe you're right. I need not sleep with Alec."

Essie's shoulders sank in relief. "I knew it. I knew you wouldn't, really."

"If you tell me what it's like," Kate grinned.

Essie smacked her in the shoulder, and Kate yelped loud enough that the instructor looked over and shook her head disapprovingly. "You brat!" Essie hissed. "You absolute hellion!"

"Please, Essie Ess. Pretty pretty please with a cherry on top and a sprinkling of brown sugar and pistachios and chocolate caramel fudge? Just one word?"

"Fine!" Essie pursed her lips. "It's… good."

"Good! That's all I get!"

"That's what you wanted. You got it. Just one word."

"Poor Eli," Kate snapped. "He's stuck with you."

"Lucky Eli."

"Lucky you, Elias."

Eli laughed. "I know. She's wonderful. She got up early and made me breakfast this morning," he bragged.

"Man… if I had a girl like that… damn," Greg whistled.

"Hey, that's my wife you're talking about!" Eli admonished.

His friend and colleague admired the picture on Eli's phone a moment longer before Eli put it away, uncomfortable with the other man ogling his wife. "She is great though. I love her."

"Lucky you," Greg shook his head again.

There was a short knock on the door, and their boss' secretary poked her head in. "Hey, Mr. Darcy, Mr. Schott. Boss wants to know if you have those packages, she asked for you to look for. They're due at the end of the day."

Elias smiled, "Yeah. Here they are, Miss Gretel."

She smiled back and took the pile of folders from him. "Just Rachel. And congrats on your marriage."

"Thank you."

"Oh, before I forget, you have a visitor in the anteroom, Mr. Darcy."

"Okay. Wave him in."

Rachel nodded and left the room. Eli saw Greg watching her and nodded for him to go. He offered to help carry some papers, and she accepted graciously. Eli nodded in satisfaction and propped his feet up on the desk. "Hello, how are you this afternoon?" he spoke generically to the person coming into his office.

"Get off you're a—I mean—butt. I'm taking you out for dinner," the person shoved Eli's feet off of the desk, and Eli nearly fell over in surprise.

"Andy!"

"Yep, let's move."

"I can't," Eli protested. "I have to finish up with my papers here, and then I have to pick up dinner for Esmeralda."

"You love talking about her and doing stuff for her, don't you?" Andy shook his head. "Come on. You're on lunch break. You can pick something up as we go. I haven't seen you in a week."

"It's three in the afternoon. What kind of lunch break!"

"The kind that means your boss' PA is beautiful and sweet," Andy said cheekily.

"You're a bad influence," Eli stood up.

"I know," he smirked.

At the restaurant he chose, Andy found a booth and ordered, waiting for the food to arrive by asking, "So what are you planning to get her for dinner?"

"I would rather take her out than get takeout," Eli mumbled. "She will have had a long day readjusting to school, and she'll want to relax. I want to do something romantic. Fast food doesn't seem right. I don't want her to even have to open the fridge."

"What's the most romantic thing you've ever done for her?" Andy asked.

Eli smiled, "I've told you about this."

"Tell me again. It's cute," Andy tossed wavy red hair out of his face and widened his eyes. "Please, please, please?"

"For crying out loud. I'd expect this from Kate but not you," Eli rolled his eyes. It's all a show. He was happy to talk about the night he proposed to Essie. The most romantic thing he could ever have prepared. He hoped that Andy might one day find a love as he had. Romance was the right way to get girls, or at least the girls he should want. And Eli fancied himself a romance expert.

Elias had picked Essie up from her home around 6:30. The sun was just setting, and dusk painted her blond hair in varying shades of perfectly spun gold. She was wearing a white dress with a pale green bow around the waist and a light-green flower over one ear. Eli got out of the car and held the door for her. He thought about leaning closer until his lips brushed over her cheek. Until his mouth caressed hers. He pulled away. "You look so beautiful, Esmeralda."

"Thank you, Eli," she bowed her head modestly and ducked into the car with perfect manners. "Where are we going?" She asked as he eased the car out of the driveway, and Essie leaned out the window the last time to wave goodbye to her mother.

Elias leaned toward her with a half-smile. He put one arm around the back of her chair. Not touching her but close enough he could. Close enough, she felt loved and protected and cherished. "Secret," he winked.

Essie pretended to pout. "Eli, come on, tell me."

"Nuh-uh. I like surprising you. You make such a cute face."

"All that flattery. You're just a regular Mr. Darcy, aren't you?" She peeked up at him through slightly lowered eyelashes, and his heart flipped.

"You know it," he managed.

She giggled. "I do, don't I?"

They pulled up to their favorite restaurant, and Eli got out of the car quickly to open her door and took her hand. They had held hands before, but still, every time they did, Essie felt butterflies take swift flight in her gut. Happy butterflies with pink- and red-heart-covered wings. Eli felt the same way and smiled reassuringly at her. She lifted her chin with an autocratic tilt, not giving way to emotion. Eli looked at the stunning, proud young woman and was once again determined to have her forever.

"You couldn't have told me we were coming to The Seine?" Essie asked puzzled. "It's my favorite restaurant. We come here often."

"Not like this," Eli insisted, drawing her hand toward him and kissing her knuckles sweetly.

"Eli…" she said shyly.

"I'm sorry," he dropped her hand.

She slowly raised it to brush away the cold air near his cheek. She touched his face gently in the cool misty evening. "It's okay."

He didn't hesitate before clasping the small gloved hands to his heart. "Thank you. Come on, let's go inside," he had to change the subject before he made a mistake and kissed the chill out of her cheeks and smothered the suspect out of her actions. He wanted her to love him. He wanted her to want him. He wanted her to trust him. And so instead of doing what he wanted to, he took her inside.

Essie felt a twinge of disappointment before she could hustle it away. She was a virtuous woman. A pure, untouched girl. She shouldn't want him to kiss her. But she wanted him to want her the way a man should want a woman. She wanted to be his, the way Eve had been

Adam's. That twinge fell away quickly when he led her into the restaurant and then past all the normal tables.

"Eli," she pulled back. "Where are you taking me?" All the warnings she had ever heard about going places alone with men—especially older men—came rushing back in a wave of worry. Whistling words of unease around her body and telling her to bring back the walls to keep people out.

"It's okay, Esmeralda," he smiled softly.

She put her hand more snuggly in his and kept following. This was Elias Darcy. He would never ever do anything to hurt her. Essie saw that Eli was following a staff member of the restaurant. The man led them to the back of the restaurant near where the doors off to the balcony seats were, but instead, he turned the other direction. He led them to a small room and left Eli to open the door.

Elias turned to her with a soft smile. "Come on, Esmeralda. I think you'll like it."

And indeed, she did. So much so she gasped and exclaimed, "Oh, gosh, Eli! It's so beautiful! I could cry!"

"Well, please don't!" he laughed at her. "I took so much time to organize it; it'd be a shame for tears to blur it all out."

Essie burst into laughter and in a moment of impulse threw her arms around his neck. Eli froze. He hadn't expected that. He slowly put his arms around her back, certain that she would be unhappy if he touched her any lower than that, as was clearly possible. He put his cheek down on the top of her head, reveling in the blond cloud.

Embarrassed by her boldness, Essie was first to pull away. "I'm sorry," she tucked a strand of blond behind her ear. "Did that… bother you?"

"Not at all! I wouldn't even mind if you did it again."

At that, Essie recoiled slightly trying to read into his intentions. True, he hadn't touched her waist inappropriately although she had immodestly given him the chance, but she was here alone with him. He wouldn't try anything… What would Mama say… She at once heard her Mama's voice in her head screeching at her to have a little fun. But then… Mama hadn't grown up in the church.

Eli saw the battle going on in her mind. He was even a little bit confused. She had to know why he had invited her here. She couldn't be that naive, after seeing all the work he had put into decorating and dressing—he was wearing a suit for crying out loud!—She had to know he was interested in her. So what's the harm in a hug?

"Do you regret it?" he asked curiously more than anything else.

"Not at all," she bowed her head demurely and did the thing Eli loved when she peeked up through her eyelashes, giving him just a glimpse of the green jewels and the appearance of a soft, shy young woman.

"So why did you apologize?"

Essie opened her mouth a few times, contemplating whether or not to tell him. She finally said, "It was very bold. I've grown up in the church, and the whole time they have told me women aren't supposed to be bold. Women should be modest and demure and never alone with a man, and God forbid touch him before they are married. I'm supposed to submit to my father, husband, boyfriend, brother and let him lead."

Eli laughed out loud, and Essie's face fell. "No, no! I'm not laughing at you! I'm laughing because my whole life I have grown up being told that a man should be careful with a woman and respectful and take our cues about what is acceptable from the woman. If she doesn't make a move, then we should definitely not."

Wrinkling her nose, Essie exclaimed, "So... I'm supposed to be demure and shy even if I wanted you to touch me, and you're not allowed to touch me unless I make the first move, which I am not allowed to do. That's so stupid!"

Eli laughed again. "Esmeralda Landry, I can't believe you. Did you just use the 'S' word!"

She tipped her chin up and looked him definitely right in the eyes, hers twinkling, speckled with humor. "Maybe I did, Elias Darcy. What will you do about it?"

"Nothing I'm allowed to," he winked.

Essie felt her heart flip with that wink. They had been courting for nearly 28 months now. Was he telling her that he liked her? She really wanted him to be. That would mean he would marry her. She was ready to be married and have a home away from her mom. With someone who would love her and take care of her.

"Come in, properly," Eli said suddenly as if he didn't know or didn't care what effect his words and actions had on her.

Essie stepped into the room and spun around to be able to see all of it. It was completely decorated like nothing she had ever seen before. Like winter and summer combined. There was a large window on one end where she could see snow flurries begin to fly, lit up by the glow of the streetlamps. The walls were draped over in swaths of blue and white cloth. Some, block colors, but others were extraordinary displays of tiny silver snowflakes or collages of little snowmen and penguins wearing ice skates.

And the flowers. Bachelor buttons, blue orchids and carnations, hydrangea and delphinium, and dozens more she had never heard of or seen. The whole room gave off auras of calm and spirituality.

Eli, suddenly at her side murmured, "Generally, blue flowers stand for loyalty, trust, intelligence, wisdom, truth, faith, and confidence and give a sense of stability, confidence, honesty, and security."

"All good things," she turned her head and smiled at him, their faces only centimeters apart.

"Yes, Esmeralda. All good things"—like you—he longed to add. But even after their brief conversation about the social rules they had each grown up respecting, he found it difficult to say something so brash.

"You're all of those good things," Essie blurted out, turning red as she did so but refusing regret. She meant it. He was all of those things.

Eli's mouth dropped open. She had stolen the words right out of his mouth. And she had been brave enough to say them while he hadn't been.

"How on earth did you find the time to decorate this place?" Essie asked, twirling carefree across the room.

Eli resisted the urge to call out to her to be careful and not to bump into anything. But he didn't think that she would really appreciate being told what to do. Instead, he just answered the question. "I got Katie and Aunt Phoebe to help."

Essie came back over and looked up at him. "It's always kind of startling for me to hear you call her that," she giggled. *"I call her Auntie Phoebe because Kate's my best friend in the world, and she was like a second mother to me. But she's actually your aunt isn't she."*

"Yeah. I mean, yes. She's my mother's sister."

At that moment, both of them were thinking about Kate, and the fact that, should they be married, Kate and Essie wouldn't just be best friends. They'd be related.

Then Essie lifted her head again and spun across the room.

Eli watched her with an interested smile. "I've never seen you like this before," he commented.

"Like what?" Essie stopped and tipped her head toward him. Her hair tumbled over her shoulder in a cascade of gold.

Eli's mouth went dry at the motion. If he didn't know her better and know that she could never possibly be a succubus, he would have called the lithe movement seductive. "Like…" he cleared his throat. "Like so relaxed and carefree."

Essie laughed. "Well, Elias. This dress just needs to be twirled in," she motioned to the flowy calf-length skirt. "Second, I am carefree and relaxed. I love being with you."

Again both of them thought at the same time I love you. But neither spoke.

Eli glanced at his watch and exclaimed, "Esmeralda, the food will be here soon. I got you a gift."

"Ooh!" she clapped her hands like a child. Eli found it charming and attractive. He wanted to take care of her. He loved buying gifts for her, and she loved getting them every time. He handed her the package in the dark blue bag, and she opened it joyfully, pulling out a book box.

She smiled and started to laugh happily. "Pride and Prejudice," she read off of the top. "I love it!"

There was the 'L' word again. The one that Eli wanted to beat himself up over every time he heard it because he felt like less of a man every time he was too shy to say those ever so important three words. "I'm glad," he answered.

The waiter knocked at the door, and Eli got up to let him in. Essie clapped again at delight in the dishes he had ordered. Both of their favorite things. Essie hadn't even known he was paying attention to what she liked best.

He served her with a smile, and she responded happily. Then things got quiet. It could have been they were hungry. It could have been they had run out of things to discuss. It could have been they were shy. But whatever the reason, they were quiet. Every now and then, one or the other would look up at the other with a face full of emotion. Full of something unexplainable. Something deeper than words.

The last dinner plate was clean, and the last bits of conversation cleaned up. Around now was the time that Eli would usually drive her home. But she didn't push the issue. She was 20 years old and living in her mother's house, and there were certain rules to abide by. She had a curfew that she respected as it was her mother's home and because she respected her mom. Besides, her mom had given her an extended curfew by two hours tonight. Essie didn't know why, but Eli apparently had known about it. In the years that they had been dating, he had never gotten her home late. He knew her curfew and respected it. But today, he had planned for later. He had ordered a dessert that only now was being paraded into the room.

He was watching her as she took a bowl of something sweet off of the tray. He took a deep breath and asked quickly before he could be too afraid to, "How do you feel about marriage?"

Essie nearly dropped her dish. "What do you mean?"

"Marriage. What do you think about it?"

Setting down her bowl and spoon, Essie propped her chin up on her hand. "Well…" she began slowly, "In the abstract, it is a relationship ordained by God through his representative on earth in which a man and a woman should leave their parents and be joined as one flesh. And in which a wife ought to submit to her husband…"

"That's not what I mean," Eli interrupted.

"That's what you asked," Essie retorted. "That's what the Bible says."

"I know, but I asked what you think," Elias pushed. "What do you think about marriage? Is it good? Does it work? Should wives be submissive?"

Essie had to think harder about that one. What could she tell him without scaring him away with her views? He was a Godly man. He would want the views of his future wife to match up with God's views. And this had to be it, right? He couldn't be thinking about marriage in terms of someone else! It had to be about her. It had to be.

"Please, Esmeralda? I want us to be able to be honest with each other and talk about the tough stuff. I want to know what you think. Honestly," Eli looked pleading at her.

"Okay," she came to a decision. If he couldn't handle her honest thoughts, they would never work out anyway. She wasn't so eager and desperate to be married that she would let herself be stifled and become someone else. She lifted

her chin defiantly. (Her signature motion of "I'm about to say something you or other people might not like," Eli thought to himself.)

"I believe that God created it to work out well. But… but even in the church, there's a half and half, 50%, success rate. My mom has been married three times. I never really knew, my father, and I hated both stepfathers. Two marriages ended when her husbands died early. She doesn't believe in divorce and neither do I, but that means that if you're in a marriage relationship, you're in it for life."

"Some marriages work out," Eli insisted. He hoped she didn't really believe that marriage was destined to fail like his cousin Kate did. She claimed she would never marry as it was too much of a hassle to divorce when it broke up. Eli was always afraid she would just end up living in sin with some cad.

"I know. I'm thinking of Aunt Phoebe and Mr. Troy. They've been together going on for 40 years. I want that. I don't think I've ever seen them argue or fight or even say a mean word to each other that wasn't in jest."

"Aunt Phoebe and Uncle Ray are a great example of what marriage should be," Eli agreed in relief. "I always wanted what my parents have. They've been together for 48 years. So close to 50. I want to spend my life with someone like that."

"Yeah. Me too," Essie nodded, suddenly seeing him in a new light. He was an absolute romantic. He just wanted to love someone who needed him. She needed him, she thought. She could be the wife he wanted. But she couldn't think of how to suggest it. She suddenly couldn't imagine him with anyone else. She wanted to be that wife. So badly.

"Esmeralda," he started in a soft tone. "C'mere," he patted the seat beside him.

She went over and was sitting close enough to him that she could smell his cologne. "Yes," she wasn't sure for what she was saying yes to.

Eli was all of a sudden holding the book box again. "Open it."

"I don't want to," she exclaimed. "The book could be damaged before I even have a chance to start reading it. Books are sacred you know."

"I know," he said, voice threaded with amusement. "Open it anyway."

She scowled at him good-naturedly and opened the box, expecting something other than a book. Inside was just a book. A beautiful glossy-covered copy of Pride and Prejudice, and it was beautiful. But it was just a book.

She looked up at him in confusion, and he said gently, "Take out the book."

Essie took out the book and laid it to the side. Underneath was a bookmark. A paper bookmark with an image on the front of Mr. Darcy from the book holding hands with Elizabeth Bennett and arching over them the words 'and they lived happily ever after.'

Lying on the bookmark was a little silver ring with a heart-cut emerald laid into it with three tiny diamonds on either side.

And then Eli was on his knee holding the ring up to her and asking, "Esmeralda Anne Maia Landry, will you live happily ever after with me as my beloved wife?"

There were tears and hugs as she fell from her chair into his arms. He brushed her tears away, demanding why she was crying, and she explained that she was so happy and she couldn't believe it was real.

He picked her up and set her back on the chair, not letting go of her hands. Leaning close and pressing their foreheads together, Eli murmured those words Essie longed to hear. "Esmeralda, I love you."

"I love you too, Eli," she whispered back.

"Your relationship is too perfect," Andy remarked later while he helped Eli look through the menu of their favorite restaurant. "Who on earth knows this much about someone else? Like… you have picked out four meals that you say she would enjoy, none of which I even knew existed, let alone were her favorites—and I've known her for 20 years longer than you. We grew up together!"

"Yeah well… she tells me lots of things that she wouldn't and shouldn't tell you, Andrew," Elias smirked. "I am her husband."

"Whatever. I'm her cousin-in-law," Andy blustered.

Eli just laughed. "Thou shalt not covet thy neighbor's wife…"

"Don't preach at me!" Andy pretended to be offended.

"Don't make eyes at my girl," he retorted.

Chapter 3

Essie smiled as she reached for the bowl of popcorn.

"Oh, my gosh, Esmeralda! You'll finish it before the movie even starts!" Eli laughed from where he was pushing play on his laptop, streaming to the TV. "I want some too!"

"So come and get it! It wasn't nice of you to leave me alone here anyway," she teased.

He hurried back and settled into the couch with her, suddenly picking her up and setting her into his lap.

"Eli!"

He buried his face in her hair and kissed her neck. "Yes? Don't say you're not more comfortable this way."

"I'm not complaining," Essie protested. "But you took my popcorn!"

He laughed and kissed her soundly as the movie began. Suddenly, he reached over and snuggled her into his chest. "Hey, gem, I love you. Did you know? I wasn't sure if I've told you often enough."

She giggled and squirmed away enough to be able to look him in the eyes. "Of course, I know, Elias. The ring, flowers, this house, the car, the fact that you brought home dinner without me having to ask… Of course, I know you love me."

"No, Esmeralda. Those are things any husband should do for his wife, regardless of what their feelings are for each other. I really, really love you. Like the kind that makes my heart flip-flop and be full of butterflies, would go through anything and give up anything for you, kind of love," he leaned down and kissed her lips gently.

Essie pulled away a little, "Eli…"

"Gem, we don't have to hide. We're married now. C'mere," he pecked her again.

"Eli, I love you too," she let herself be swept away in a wave of caresses.

A week later, Essie reveled in the warm bed later than usual. She wasn't punctual on the best of days, but today, her earliest class started at half past noon, and she wanted to make the best of her time at home. When she woke up at her normal time, she smiled and rolled over, going back to sleep.

That same day, Eli woke up late. Essie was still asleep and smiling in her slumber as if she didn't have a care in the world. Eli felt a jolt of irritation but capped it quickly. Not her fault. He kissed her forehead briefly and pulled himself out from under the blankets. Eli stumbled toward his closet trying to, with sleep-filled eyes, pick out a shirt and tie that matched. Again he looked toward Essie. It was a task that Eli found trying and tough but necessary. Half the guys at his work would show up in plaid shirts with paisley ties and think everything was okay. Eli knew what didn't match, but the problem was finding the things that did. But Essie wasn't up, and Eli didn't want to wake her. He showered and went back to the problem of the outfit. He glanced at the clock on the wall and bit back a curse. If he needed 10 minutes for breakfast and 16 minutes to drive to work, he had a minute left to get dressed before he was late.

He grabbed a shirt and tie that he was pretty sure he had worn the week before, and Essie had picked out. He was pretty certain it matched, but looking again in the mirror, he wasn't quite as convinced. He rubbed his temples, feeling a headache coming on. Don't think about it anymore. He counseled himself. He ran out to the kitchen, hoping at least that Essie had made him breakfast as she had been doing every morning since they were married. But, of course, she was still asleep, and there was nothing for him. In fact, there was a stack of dishes in the sink that had to be dug through in order to get a clean bowl and spoon.

Eli was not afraid of dishes. He had done his fair share of them while living at home. The oldest of nine children, no one was allowed to hate chores, not even the boys. Eli on a normal day would have had no problem washing the dishes before going to work and give Essie a break, but he was late. And he just wanted to have breakfast and hurry about it. He reached into the pile and pulled out a bowl. As he did so, the precarious tower of glass groaned and gave way. There was a loud crack and then a sharp pain as a plate cracked and sliced across the back of his hand. Eli cried out, wrenching his hand away and running it under cold water. He looked at the clock again, knowing that he should already be driving but in the logical part of his head knowing that he couldn't leave with blood streaming down his forearm and no breakfast.

He fairly sprinted back to the bathroom leading off their bedroom. He paused long enough to feel a twist of fury that Essie was still sleeping peacefully. Then he headed into the bathroom. He washed off the arm and with the other one awkwardly wrapped a bandage around his hand. It would have been way easier to with another pair of hands. Eli debated whether or not he should wake her up to help him but couldn't bring himself to do it. She deserved her sleep. He knew that school was hard for her and that she was doing the best she could. Besides, none of what had happened today was actually her fault.

Eli walked past her again, conscious of the fact he was still late and needed to have breakfast. He went to the kitchen and opened the fridge looking for the easiest quick thing he could find.

When Essie woke up, she lay drowsily in the bed a few moments longer. She had nothing to do all morning. She stretched lazily and curled up again in the warm blankets. Unexpected, there was a loud crash from the kitchen followed by a screamed curse and angry steps toward the bedroom yelling, "Esmeralda Darcy!"

Eyes opened wide in shock; she swung her feet out of bed. As her feet dropped to the floor, Eli came stomping into the room dripping goo from every orifice. Her eyes were fixated on the floor, and she frowned, "Why is there blood on the carpet?"

His answer was silent yet palpable simmering anger. Essie looked up and swallowed. "Eli, what's going on...? Shouldn't you be at work?"

"You know the damn pitcher of maple syrup that you left open in the fridge like a week ago! The one I told you *not to leave!*" he snapped. "Well guess what. This morning, I opened the fridge and the whole damn container fell on me. And I know I should be at work, Esmeralda. But I think it's pretty clear that I can't go like this," he seethed.

Essie looked at him, dripping in syrup, hand bandaged clumsily and leaking blood, tie and shirt not matching at all. She bit her lip and stood up, reaching out a hand toward him. He jerked away, growling between clenched teeth, "I have to go."

Overwrought and still sleepy, shocked from having being woken so suddenly, Essie burst into tears.

Eli looked at her, and his face softened. At the same time, he couldn't find it in himself to apologize or disperse any of his anger. "Shit, now you're crying," he rubbed the back of his head trying to make a decision and then walked out of the room.

Essie crawled back to bed and lay there crying for the better part of the next half hour. When she got out of bed later, she wandered to the kitchen. The whole sorry story was laid out there. From the broken glass littering the floor and sink to the sticky syrup on the floor and the pitcher all in one piece while her husband's day was shattered. Essie felt like falling to the floor again and sobbing her heart out. She didn't. She got up and washed the dishes and counter until they sparkled. She scrubbed the floor frantically and in a fervor then mopped it too. She paced feverishly through the house and found it in perfect condition. She couldn't even locate a basket of laundry to be folded or washed.

All the while she was thinking about what had happened and what could have. She should've been up on time. She should've helped Eli get up on time. She should've helped him get dressed and made him breakfast as she normally did. It wasn't his fault that he depended on her. She should've had the dishes washed so he never cut himself. She should've been up to help him wash and bandage his hand if it had happened anyway. She should've listened to him and put the damned cover on the damned pitcher.

She spied her phone, and before she thought twice, she had it in her hand and was speed-dialing her mom.

Kyra picked up with a note of concern. "Hey, Es. Everything okay?"

"Mama?" Essie started and choked on a sob. "We had an argument and…"

"Oh, honey… these things happen. Tell me about it, and we'll figure it out," her mom answered sweetly. And with a note of evasiveness, Essie noticed, as if she wasn't fully paying attention.

"Mama, I wanna come home," Essie whimpered.

"Es… honey… you have to work things out with him."

"Can I just come visit?"

There is a pause and then, "Of course, Esmeralda."

"Thank you."

"It's no problem Es… only…"

Essie had already hung up, not wanting to know what that was for. She quickly got dressed and slipped a purse over her shoulder. She would have to text Kate to take notes for her. The class was going to wait.

Essie was met with conflicting feelings as she waited at the front door of what used to be her and her mom's house. And the occasional visiting nuisance but generally just for her and her mama. Now she felt like a stranger standing in front of the door. She hesitated, not sure if she should knock.

Before she could make up her mind, the door was pulled open. Essie looked up, expecting to see her mom's smiling face framed by her puff of brown hair and a colorful scarf. She was met with the creature she wanted to see least at the moment.

"Esmeralda. Good to see you."

"Can't say the same, Clayton," Essie snapped pushing past him into the house, noting in satisfaction his curled lip at her words. "Where's my mom?"

"I think she just stepped around the corner. Are you just here to join us for lunch? Can I get you something?" he asked smoothly, gracing her with a cool smile.

"I came to see my mother. Why are you here?"

"I live here now."

Essie snorted. "No, she didn't invite you here…" Her heart started to sink. She wouldn't have. Would she?

Clay nodded. "Of course, she did. Once you moved out. I seem to remember that you were the one who refused to accept me into the family, but like it or not, I am married to your mother," he appraised her arrogantly.

Essie huffed and threw her boots at the door, collapsing into a chair in the living room. She flung her purse after her shoes. "If this day gets any worse, I'm calling hell to ask if they have an exchange program."

Clay remained standing with his ever-present smirk, "Sugar, that's a new level of melodramatic, even for you."

"Go to hell, Clay."

"Esmeralda," he rolled her name around his mouth as he settled against a wall. "I already know I'm going there. It must be a sin how much I just love your mama. At this point, it's just go big or go home."

"Did she say what time she'd be back?" Essie ignored him.

"Hmm… now that you mention it, I don't believe she did. I'm afraid you're stuck with me for the time being, darlin'."

"God, kill me or kill him. Preferably him. I'll even help!" Essie mumbled as she got up and stalked around the house. Knowing Clay, her mom was just in her room listening to music, didn't hear her come in and he's enjoying snipping with her.

"I heard that, Miss Landry."

"You were supposed to, Clay," Essie flung back. "And it's Mrs. Darcy to you."

"Oh, right. Forgive me for forgetting. Has that happened already? I recall I wasn't invited to the wedding."

"No one would want a—someone like you!—at their wedding."

Clay wasn't lying. Kyra wasn't home. Essie resigned herself to sitting in the kitchen, angry and heartbroken about the fight with Eli and wanting so badly for Clay to jump off a cliff. Finally, the door opened. Essie was up in a flash and met her mom at the door, grabbing a few bags of groceries away from her mom who was handing them off to Clay. She scowled at him, and he backed off, making a face back at her.

Essie glared at her mom. "Mama, I didn't know you weren't home. Or that you had company."

"I didn't expect you over so soon, but anyway, Clayton's not a company, Esmeralda. He lives here."

"I was just telling her, Kyra, that…" Clay interrupted.

Essie fired at him immediately, "Do I get bonus points if I pretend I care?"

"Esmeralda, sarcasm isn't nice."

"Mama, you must understand. Sarcasm is the body's natural defense against stupidity," Essie raised her eyebrows defensively.

"Sounds like something Kate would say," Kyra responded wearily settling into her favorite chair. "It's not a pretty look on you."

Essie knelt beside her. "Mama. I came to see you. I don't want *him* listening."

"Sit in a chair properly, Esmeralda," Kyra instructed.

Essie obeyed, sulky and even more black in mood as Clay went over to her Mom's right-hand side, taking her hand and kissing it.

Kyra saw the faces of both her husband and her daughter and sighed, "Clayton, Esmeralda did come to see me. Could you maybe put the kettle on?"

He nodded without snapping at Essie, and her expression softened as he left. As soon as he was out of sight, Kyra looked sharply at her daughter and pronounced, "Esmeralda, I thought we were past this. You're older now. And a married woman in your own rights. Surely, you can see why I would want my husband to live with me. You're a bright girl; please make an effort."

"Mama… he's insufferable!"

"Esmeralda, you're an adult. I expect better. At least make an effort to be polite. While you're at my house? Manners won't kill you."

Clay appeared at the fringe of the room and supplied, "What doesn't kill you makes you stronger?"

"What doesn't kill me might make me kill you?" she quipped without hesitation.

Kyra raised her eyebrows, and Essie hung her head. "Sorry, mama. I can't help it!"

"And you, Clayton, I thought you were making tea?" Kyra looked at him meaningfully.

"Kettle's on, not much for me to do right now," he shrugged.

"Clayton…"

"I think I'm just going to head out and see some friends," he nodded to Kyra and bowed sardonically in Essie's direction. "Until later, Kitty. Mrs. Princess Darcy."

"Don't answer, Esmeralda," her mother ordered.

"Mama, I don't know what to do!" Essie wailed.

Kyra got up patiently and went briefly to the kitchen coming back with two mugs of steaming mint and ginger. "We're going to need tea," she settled back into her armchair and handed Essie a cup. "So tell me what happened."

"I made a mess of everything," she whispered, blinking back tears.

"Esmeralda, tell me what happened unbiased."

Essie stared into her mug as she related the story to her. Kyra listened quietly, without adding any input at all. At the tail of the tale, she leaned back in her chair and looked at Essie honestly. "Esmeralda, you are partly at fault."

Having come to this same conclusion earlier on her own, Essie still bristled at the accusation. "I know, Mama… I know. I already thought about all of this. I should have been up earlier and…"

Kyra held up a no-nonsense hand. "That's not what I mean. And Esmeralda Anna Maia, if you came here to wallow in your guilt, you came to the wrong place. I can help you find solutions, but we won't be making more of a mess by soothing in self-loathing."

"Yes, Mama," Essie hung her head. "So which parts were my fault?"

"You tell me," Kyra smiled slightly.

Essie thought through the story again. "I guess… I guess I should have put the cover on the syrup."

"That would have been a very good place to start," Kyra nodded. "What else."

Essie shook her head, "I don't know."

"You didn't think about it long enough."

"Mama, I don't want to play this game anymore. I'm not a little girl."

"I know that, Esmeralda. That's why you need to figure out some of this on your own. You're a married adult. You need to go home and apologize and talk to your husband about what we talked about today and work through these problems. So what else."

Close to tears after a further minute of study, Essie looked to her mother. "Mama, I don't know! Please help me."

Kyra got up and left her for a few minutes while she refilled her mug. When she came back, Essie had cleaned her face and blown her nose. "Okay. So it would seem to me like your husband had a bad morning. You could have helped it by having put the cover on the syrup pitcher. Maybe you could have done the dishes. Probably you should have, but the rest of the morning was not all your fault."

"But Mama…"

"Esmeralda. The rest of the morning was not all your fault. There were a few big things you could have done differently and better, however. First, when it became apparent that he was having a rough time, you reacted very badly."

"What do you mean?"

"He came into your room upset, and what did you do?"

"I… cried?"

"Yes, Esmeralda. He didn't need that. That's why he walked away," she screwed up her face briefly. "He shouldn't have. But he did. Because he didn't know how to deal with how you were dealing. You need to talk to him. And you need to apologize."

"Mama…"

"Esmeralda," Kyra made a face known to Essie as don't fight with me on this one. I'm right, and you know it.

"I know you're right, Mama."

"Good. Not get home and make dinner."

Essie stood and kissed her mom on the cheek, and Kyra pulled her into a hug.

"And one last thing," Kyra called as Essie put on her shoes and reached for the door.

"Yes, Mama?"

"Don't be rude to Clay when you go out."

Essie stepped outside, and there he was, loitering around the corner with a magazine in his hand and no other reason for being there.

"Hey, sugar, have a nice evening."

Essie wrinkled her nose. "If I find out you were eavesdropping, I'll…"

"You'll what. Smite me with your magic of millennial? Cute, sweetheart, but unnecessary. I wasn't listening. Although, as your father…"

"*Step*-father."

"Whatever. Just so it's on record, Esmeralda, your mama loves me more than you could ever realize. I'm in control here. I'm the master of the house and most of the time of her. So if I were you, I'd watch my attitude the next time I wanted to come around."

"I hate you, Clayton," Esmeralda said coolly as she climbed into the car.

"Just hate me from a distance, sugar," he leaned over and shut the door for her with a self-righteous sneer.

What had started out as a bad day got worse. Eli changed into a cleaner, but a terribly wrinkled shirt and tie in his car as he drove. He stopped at a diner to get a bad breakfast. When he got to work, his business partner was late and Rachel was off, leaving him to fend with the boss' other assistant, a woman named Nyota Notley who was even younger than he and useless.

"Miss Notley!" he called again from his cubicle. "Miss Notley," he called again with a tempered tone.

She walked into the room all flustered and upset. "Yes, Mr. Darcy? What can I do for you?"

"These aren't the packets that you said they were. Are they the right ones, or are you confused?"

"They are… I mean… they ar-aren't… I mean… uh…"

Eli held back the temptation to throw them at her bumbling head. "Miss Notley, why don't you take them back and sort through them? I'll get back to you after my lunch break."

She looked relieved at the idea of getting away from him and having a chance to gather her thoughts. "Yes, sir! That's a great idea. Can I get you anything? Before you… go?"

Eli swept past her, putting on his coat as he went.

"Okay, bye, sir! I'll see you later!"

Mrs. Grail took a half step out of her office. "Nya, please don't shout."

"Sorry, Ma'am," Nyota exclaimed anxiously.

Mrs. Grail tipped her head to the side as they watched Eli march out in such a flurry. "Is he alright, you think?" She questioned. Eli was one of her best workers and had been with the company since they started up. He had worked there as an intern when he was 16, working his way through the ranks, using the job to pay for his university so he could move his way up to the position he had now. Mrs. Grail had a comfortable and almost maternal kind of feeling for him.

"I don't know, Ma'am. He was as polite as ever, but he did seem a bit…"

"A bit what, Nya?"

"Bothered."

"Okay. Has he gotten through those papers I sent over?"

"No, ma'am. I… I gave him the wrong folders."

"*That's* why he was testy," Mrs. Grail laughed, settling a hand on the younger woman's shoulder. "Don't worry about it, Nyota."

Eli sat outside of the building in his car. The keys were in the ignition, but he had yet to turn them. The GPS was open on his phone, but he hadn't searched anything. His hands were poised over the steering wheel but not touching it. He had no idea what he was doing.

He knew he should have reacted better this morning. Okay, sure, maybe, Essie should have put the cover back on the pitcher, but he should have done the dishes last night when she was tired and went to bed. It was no one's fault that he cut his hand. It's his own fault that he slept in. But he took it out on her. And when she was clearly upset after being woken up out of bed by being yelled at, he had left her crying in their bedroom. The room of their house that should have been a safe haven.

His first instinct was to call his mother. She would know what to do, what to say to solve everything. He folded his arms and leaned on his steering wheel. It honked suddenly, and he jumped back. He was a grown man, for God's sake. He shook his head. He wasn't going to go running back to his parents at the first sign of danger. He was good at taking care of himself. And he would take care of her, too.

Going around the house, Essie carefully lit all the candles. They barely lit the house, so, on afterthought, she turned on a lamp as well. She had done as her mother suggested. She had made dinner and set the table and put on a clean dress. When the door opened, she should have been ready. Instead, she felt a spasm of fear. What if it wasn't enough? Eli, at the bottom of the stairs, was in a white shirt and a green tie. Her favorite color.

"Hey, Esmeralda," Eli looked up shyly. "Can I come up?"

"Of course!"

"Right um…" he looked at the package in his hands. "I brought ice cream?"

"I love ice cream," Essie smiled as he came up the stairs and took his hand.

He looked in the rooms that Essie had decorated and turned his head to her with a smile. "It's all beautiful."

"Thank you."

"I brought you flowers," Elias offered them.

Essie took them and thanked him, settling them into a vase as they retreated back to the awkward silence.

Essie's blond curls tumbled over her shoulder and over part of her face. Eli wanted so badly to know what she was thinking. What all that hair was hiding. He wanted to apologize but couldn't find the words.

He gestured around to the dinner she had prepared. "It all looks really great…"

"What do you say we start with ice cream?" Essie suggested. "What kind did you get?"

"Mint chocolate chip," Elias answered with a ghost of a smile.

"My favorite," Essie exclaimed. "Green chocolate chip!"

Eli nodded at her and laughed, "Yes."

Essie looked at the table, elegantly set in crystal with serviettes folded into swans and everything pristine. "Do you mind if…"

"Living room?" Eli pleaded. "I was thinking the exact same thing."

They settled onto the couch with the tub of ice cream between them, each with a spoon. Halfway through the box of frozen heaven, Essie sighed and impulsively rested her shoulder on Eli's shoulder. "So… we kind of have two options here. I can consider myself bribed by ice cream, and we can just forgive each other silently and move on, or we can talk about it."

"Talk about what? I don't know what you mean?" Eli asked innocently, reaching over and tugging on a long blond twist.

"Really?" Essie's heart leaped.

"Not really, love. We've gotta talk about it."

Essie whimpered and fell over sideways into Eli's lap. "I'm sorry!"

"For what! It wasn't your fault! I'm sorry!"

"I'm sorry for not putting the cover on the syrup when you told me and for reacting so badly when you confronted me about it. I should have seen that you were having a bad day. You didn't need to deal with an emotional wife on top of it all," Essie said earnestly.

"I'm sorry for taking my bad day out on you. I knew you were tired the night before. I should've washed the dishes, and even anyway, it wasn't anyone's fault that I cut myself or that I can't match a tie and a shirt," Eli answered.

"Friends again?" Essie asked.

Eli bent and kissed her mouth gently. "Always. I love you."

"I love you too."

They retired to the elegant dining room and took their places. Eli took a good look at the table and picked up his place mat full of dishes pulling it around to beside Essie's place. "I don't want to be that far from you," he grinned.

"I missed you today," Essie said with a note of surprise. "I didn't know we had gotten so close."

"I missed you too, and I certainly hope we've gotten so close. We're going to be married forever."

"Can this be our last fight ever?"

"That sounds perfect."

That night, Essie was super careful to do everything right. All the dishes were washed and put away, which even turned out to be fun when Eli joined in. They put on some music and danced the dishes from sink to shelf.

The next morning, Essie woke up early and picked an outfit with Eli so they match. She chose a light-blue, flowy, off-the-shoulder blouse with ruffles all over the top. She paired it with a dark navy-blue pencil skirt. She pulled her hair back into a white ribbon. Eli came out of the closet and held up two ties to his collar. "Gem, which one?"

The first is dark blue with black swirls and, the second, solid black. "Neither?" Essie said helpfully. "Hold on. I swear I saw one better," Essie disappeared into the closet space and came back out a few minutes later with a light-blue tie, speckled with tiny white birds. "This one."

"Aren't I lucky to have such a fantastic girl?" he put his arm around her waist and drew him to her, kissing her soundly.

Essie almost melted under his hands, feeling more awake than she ever had.

Eli noticed and held her tighter. She let out a little gasp as his lips move to her neck and over her shoulder. "Esmeralda," he sighed against her soft skin.

"Eli," she mewled as he gathered her to him. She closed her eyes as his hands wandered.

"Eli," she whispered again. She forced herself to take a step back. "Not now, Eli. We'll be late for school and work," Essie leaned back and deftly knotted the tie around his throat, folding the collar perfectly.

"How did you know how to do that?" he asked, intrigued. He really liked it. He liked how domestic she was. That she was happy to stay home and cook and clean and pick matching outfits with him.

"I practiced," she winked.

"Sexy," Eli winked and drew her close again.

"Eli," she pressed him away. "Come on."

Eli didn't let his emotions show on his face, but he was very disappointed. At first, he had just thought that she was shy and needed to warm up to him, but it was quickly becoming apparent that Essie really didn't share his want— his need—for physical touch. She liked it when he did stuff for her and bought her little gifts and when they just spent time together, but it wasn't as important to her to snuggle and hear the words I love you... the things that were necessities for him.

He thought about it as he started driving to work that morning. Was what he felt wrong? It wasn't always sexual affection he was looking for; he wasn't sex-addicted, but sometimes he just wanted to hug her or hold her hand. He just liked having her near. But, every now and then, when he would approach her looking for kisses or less, like trying to hold her hand for crying out loud, she would brush him away and do serviceable things. Like today! When he reached to kiss her, she distracted him by tying his tie! He really did love those little deeds of love, but he wanted to hear her say I love you instead of having to always say it first.

He wondered if he should bring it up to her. Then he wondered if him talking about his feelings would be a turnoff for her. It might be a new century; there might already be 16 editions of the iPhone released, but he had portrayed himself as the most manly of men to Essie from the start. Would she want him any differently? If she knew how sensitive he really was?

For Essie, thinking time wasn't driving to school. When she drove, she was already stressed enough trying to focus and get to class in one piece. Her thinking time was lunch with Kate. Today, she flopped onto her stomach at the end of summer grass and stared at her wedding ring, brown paper bag lunch lying beside her. She crossed her ankles and looked at the sparkly emeralds and diamonds and then the simple gold band above it. "I don't know what's wrong with him, Kate," she sighed.

"I don't know what's wrong with you," Kate shrugged, sitting up cross-legged beside her friend and looking together quite like the tableau of a preppy high school recess. "You haven't eaten any lunch yet, and it's 1 pm."

"Katelyn! I am having marital issues!" Esmeralda rolled over and flopped onto her back, holding a hand above her to block the sun.

"Okay, so solve them!" Kate said matter-of-factly. "What's wrong?"

Essie sighed. "He's just so… touchy," she wrinkled her nose. "I know that it's my Christian wife's duty to let him…"

"Horse-crap."

"And so mostly I do…"

"Bull-crap."

"But sometimes I wish that he would just help me make breakfast in the morning or… or… more… less… touchy things," Essie growled. "I mean, how am I supposed to know if he married me for me? Or if he married me because he wants my body. I mean, he says I love you all the time. But, words are empty, right? Actions, though, actions are not. He's just… such a man."

"All due respect… but that's a load of crap!" Kate exclaimed cheerfully.

"Katie!"

"Es. I'm serious. So you two express love in different ways. So talk about it."

"I don't think he's the 'talk about emotions' type. Like I said. He's a *man*."

"Lot of men talk about their feelings," Kate countered.

"Not the ones like him," Essie shook her head. "He's a cook steak on a grill in the middle of winter cause I'm a guy kind of man."

"Yeah, I know, Es. I grew up with him."

"So there you go. You know!"

"When we were growing up, he was such a cute, sensitive little guy. I think all that sensitivity is still there. Just buried down."

"You're wrong, Kate. He's so emotionally stable I feel like pudding."

"Nice allusion," Kate grimaced. "Now. What do you have for lunch? I'm done mine, and I'm still hungry."

"I don't know," Essie turned onto her stomach again, reveling in the sun's rays.

"How do you not know?"

"Eli packed it."

"Your husband packed you lunch. Seriously!" Kate screeched.

"Could you keep it down!" Essie blushed. "We packed each other's lunches today. A surprise for each other."

"Oh, God," Kate groaned. She grabbed Essie's brown paper bag and opened it. Instead of a sandwich or bag of cookies, the first thing she found was a slip of paper. Unfolding it, she found six lines of flowery cursive. "Oh. My God!" she squealed and read it aloud. "To Esmeralda, the sun of my life";

From dusk till dawn, I'm there.
From the rays of the sun to the glow of the moon, you're there.
From every sunrise to every shooting star, we're there.
And even after the sky falls, we always will be,
Until the end of time.

"Esmeralda Darcy! He writes you *poetry*!"

Essie blushed and grabbed the slip of paper from Kate. "Give me that!"

"And you say that he doesn't show emotions," her cousin-in-law chortled.

"Kate."

"Essie," she mimicked, chomping her way through the package of cookies that she had found buried in the bottom of the lunch bag.

Essie sat up and glared.

Kate shrugged. "What? If you're looking for any redeemable qualities, I don't have any," she smirked.

"You're insane, Katelyn."

"Insanity runs in my family. It practically gallops! Have you met my cousin?" she quipped wickedly.

Eli was only one drooping eyelash from being completely asleep. When the door banged open, his head flew off of the keyboard in response to the intrusion. His partner and right-hand man, Greg, stepped in and perched on the edge of his desk. "Hey, Elias, wakey wakey. You up late last night?" he asked suggestively.

Eli closed his laptop, not gently. "Slept fine. Thank you for asking," he snapped.

"Brr," Greg hugged himself. "That was icy. Touch a nerve, did I?"

"I don't really want to talk about it," Eli brushed him off, reaching to open the computer again.

Greg put a hand on top of it. "Hey, Eli, you can tell me everything, okay?"

"Just some tension with the wife."

"You mean the wife of 4 weeks?"

"That's the one. Just some difference of opinion."

"The kind that means you wish you would have slept poorly last night," Greg said knowingly.

Eli looked at him with a bit of surprise.

"I know stuff," Greg said, taking mock offense.

"Mmhmm," Elias laughed a bit. "Hey, you still looking for a girl? I have three-quarters of a mind to set you up with my little cousin."

"Tempting," Greg laughed. "But come on, a cousin of yours? She's probably crazy!"

"Hey! I'm not crazy!" Eli retorted, playfully cuffing him on the shoulder.

Eli did not confide in Greg. They *were* friends, but not that close, and Eli wasn't sure if he should be getting advice from a non-Christian single man who believed in divorce more than he did in marriage. He distracted him with some reports that Mrs. Grail wanted done, and they didn't bring it back up. Greg, however, wanted to talk about some other stuff.

At quarter to six, Eli realized that he had to leave in about 20 minutes if he wanted to be on time to meet his next appointment; of course, he did. As he started to pack up, Greg caught his attention.

"Eli, I've been thinking…"

"A dangerous pastime," he answered, not really thinking much about it.

"Nah, Elias. I have a proposal for you."

"Okay, shoot," Eli turned back and propped his feet on the desk. Something in his friend's voice made him listen. He wasn't a serious guy by nature, so his out-of-the-blue wanting to talk caught Eli's attention.

"I was thinking of leaving BlueCo," Greg began slowly.

"Why?" Eli demanded.

"I want to start my own legal firm."

"Uh… wow! Well… that's a big decision," Eli started.

"I want you to partner with me, 50/50, and help me start up," Greg said earnestly.

Eli thought about it for a few moments, getting ready to shake his head when Greg exclaimed, "Don't tell me now. I know it's a huge shift. Think about it."

Eli shook his head anyway. "I don't think that now is a good time for me. I like the idea but… you know I've been at BlueCo for 17 years. I like it here. But I've always dreamed of having my own legal firm. But now… I don't think so."

"Okay. Think about it, hey?" Greg asked.

"Of course," Elias clapped him on the back.

Needless to say, there was much on his mind by the time he got in the car to meet with Andy. As usual, they met at a little cafe for dinner before carpooling to the church for a prayer meeting. Andy hugged him tightly before they went inside. "How are you doing, Brother?"

Eli smiled, "I'm here, aren't I?"

"You'd tell me if something was wrong, right?"

"Course," he said smoothly, settling into a booth.

Kneeling in a circle with his church family later that night, Eli prayed once more that God would bless his marriage and keep him pure. He prayed that he would understand her better and be able to love her in a way she would respond to.

Essie sat alone that evening. Waiting for Eli to get home, she cooked and cleaned and cooked breakfast for the next morning and then sat nervously on the couch. The clock ticked past seven, and she let herself feel the first fingers of fear crawling out from all the black corners and cracks. The darkness crept over her body, and cold hands grabbed her. She startled and jumped up. In a flash of childlike angst, she went around the house and turned on all the lights.

Where was he? Essie frantically called his office. The secretary said that she was just packing up, and no, she hadn't seen Elias since he left the office around 5:30. In tears, Essie called Eli's phone another half a dozen times.

Essie fell into a restless sleep, woken every few moments by nightmares. She imagined him flat in the middle of a road, tied up… kidnapped… murdered… or being tortured. Each time she woke up, it was with tears in her eyes and racked with sobs.

When the door opened, Essie jumped off the couch and crept to the kitchen, grabbing a kitchen knife.

The intruder walked up the stairs with heavy steps. When the shadow moved into the kitchen and turned on the lights, Essie tightened her grip on the blade. She imagined the same man who had kidnapped and murdered her husband coming for her. Tears silently slid down her cheeks when she thought that this was how she was going to die. Alone and with no one knowing what happened to her. She couldn't believe it. Widowed at 22, after barely more than a month of marriage. She needed to tell him that she loved him one more time.

"Esmeralda?"

Essie looked up into the face of Elias Darcy. She knew that in a typical love story, she was supposed to be both relieved and furious. She was supposed to kiss him lovingly and scold him, giddy with alleviation. Instead, she felt hundreds of more emotions; most of all, the desire to be in his arms. She got up too quickly, and the room spun around her. As fast as she had stood to be with him, the room went black, and she collapsed in a faint.

Eli caught her, grunting under dead weight and moving to kneel, cradling her head on his lap. Her hair spilled in copious waves of blond tresses over her head and shoulders while a few strands mingled with fallen tears. Eli wiped away the tears and bent as if to kiss the sleeping beauty awake.

She stirred, moving her hands to her head with a whimper. Eli bent over her again, whispering her name, calling to her over and over again hoping his voice would break her trance.

When Essie opened her eyes, Eli wept with her in relief. Different problems, different reasons, but the two of them crying together on the linoleum of the kitchen. Then Essie sat up and demanded, "Where were you? I was worried sick!"

Eli looked at her with absolute honest confusion. "What do you mean?"

"This evening. Where were you?" Essie cried.

Eli looked at her strangely and brushed the hair off of her forehead. "Don't you remember? It's Tuesday? Did you hit your head when you fainted?"

"I did not. And what's Tuesday have to do with it?" Essie said coldly.

"On Tuesdays, Andy and I go to prayer meeting. We always have," Eli answered slowly.

"You never told me," Essie threw her arms around his neck, and Eli wasn't sure if she was hugging him or trying to choke him out.

"I didn't think I had to spell it out. I've been going since we met. I figured you knew."

"I was so scared…" Essie trailed off into worrying sobs again.

Eli cuddled her to him, "Shh, shh… Hey, it's okay!" He stroked her hair.

Essie pulled back and slapped his chest, "I thought you were dead!" Her oscillation drove her to once again slap his chest before falling onto him again.

"I'm sorry?" Eli ventured, sure that he had to say something to rectify events, but wasn't sure what she wanted to hear. Maybe just knowing that he was there and everything was alright would be enough for her. He pulled her more fully into his lap and hugged her tightly. Feeling her soft body against him, he sighed and instinctively reached around her little waist, playing with the fabric hem of the flouncy blouse.

Essie suddenly slapped his hands away furiously. "You can't seduce your way out of this, Mr. Darcy," she snapped and jumped up, marching to their bedroom. In the room, she stripped quickly and climbed under the quilts, simmering so that she might be worried the sheets would ignite. Men. Only thinking about one thing.

Still, on the tiled floor, Eli fell into a cross-legged position and dropped his arms helplessly. Women! She was impossibly emotional and couldn't be understood.

That was the first night that they hadn't cuddled to sleep since they were married. Around midnight, Essie woke up shivering in her thin nightgown and facing toward the outside of the bed alone. She rolled slightly and stared up at the roof she couldn't see, thinking of the husband she couldn't see on the other side of the bed. Both far and unattainable without some sacrifice. To get to Eli, she had to sacrifice her pride.

His side of the bed creaked, and his breathing was suddenly a little less even; a little less deep. "Esmeralda, you awake?" he whispered.

She had a brief and bloody argument with herself. Both armies surrendered, and Essie murmured back, "Yes."

"I'm sorry I didn't tell you where I was," he continued softly. "I'm sure you were afraid and then angry. And I wasn't much help. And your emotions were rightfully so."

"Thank you for validating my feelings," Essie remarked dryly.

"That wasn't the right thing to say, was it?" Eli sighed mournfully.

"Not even close. I don't need your validation."

"What do you need?"

"Hold me," Essie murmured. She scooted over to the center of the bed where the mattress was cold but Eli's arms around her were warm.

"Why did you faint?" Eli asked.

Essie was silent. "I really don't know. Maybe just overwrought? Funny, I'm really not the shrinking daisy type. I've never fainted a day in my life!"

"What's it like?"

"Weird. All of a sudden, everything is black and spinning, and then it's all still, and then it's like waking up from a quick nap with no recollection of how long it's been," Essie giggled.

"Are you okay now?"

"Oh, yes, perfectly," she smiled.

"What do you need? Can I do anything to be sure?" he pressed worriedly. She really didn't seem to be the shrinking violet type. Or the kind to be that emotional. Maybe it was just her woman time.

"Just hug me," Essie said content.

"So you aren't disgusted by my hugs?" he asked, mostly joking. The elbow he got in the gut in exchange for his insolence was not joking. "Sorry. It's just that sometimes, you want me to touch you and hold you, and other times, you push me away."

"There's a time and a place, Elias."

"How am I supposed to know?" he demanded.

She turned her head toward him and even in the dark he could feel her scowl. "Oh, I don't know. You could ask me?"

Elias rolled his eyes. "What do you need?"

"Without attitude," Essie glared.

"Esmeralda, gem, what do you need?" Eli felt a sudden memory jolt at the words. His father was perpetually asking his mother what she wanted. He had grown up thinking it was because he was a pushover and couldn't figure things out for himself. Now he felt why. His father probably had gotten tired of the mixed signals and signs around the first month of marriage.

"Right now?" Essie asked. "Right now I need cuddles."

"I can cuddle you," Eli said in relief. He wanted cuddles too.

"I know," Essie snipped. She softened as his arms came around her, and they gently made love. "Thank you," she whispered.

About an hour later as they basked in each other, Eli cleared his throat, having worked up enough nerve to ask, "Is it your... um... woman time?"

"What do you mean?" Essie said dangerously calmly.

"Are you, umm, menstruating?"

Essie hit him in the face with a pillow before he could take a breath, having completed the sentence. "I can be as mad as I want with no reason! I don't have to be on my period!" she exclaimed. "I rule my hormones, not the other way around!"

"Umm… having grown up with six sisters and Katelyn, I might have to disagree…" he attempted tentatively.

She hit him in the face with a pillow again, and he turned back to his, burying his face and laughing.

Chapter 4

"Esmeralda, come on!" Eli banged once again on the bathroom door. "We're going to be late! I refuse to be late! I'm going to leave without you!" he called helplessly. It was an empty threat, and Essie knew it. He couldn't arrive at church without his pretty, young wife at his side.

Essie came waltzing out of the bathroom with a towel around her body and one holding all her blonde hair up off of her face. She shed the towel and stepped into her church dress, turning her back to Eli. "Zip?"

He did her up and then sat back against the bed with a groan as she proceeded to do up her hair. "We could have taken half the time and half the water if we had taken my suggestion," he tapped his watch.

Essie flipped her hair over her shoulder to give him a dirty look. He had earlier suggested that they shower together and had been shot down with a vicious, "Not on the *Sabbath*, Elias! Pray God has mercy on your male soul."

Essie stepped into her heels and spun a little twirl for Eli. "Tada! Ready."

"And only 20 minutes off schedule," he grimaced, tossing his suit jacket over her porcelain shoulders.

"I'm not cold, Eli," Essie put her nose in the air, laughing as she passed him, pecking him on the lips fondly.

"You will be," he muttered. "You always are and you never bring your own sweater."

At the church, Eli proved to be right as Essie was instantly freezing and refused to give the jacket back. They sat together in a middle front row, their families providing a framed backdrop behind them. Showcasing the new couple as they knelt and prayed and held hands and shared a hymnal and sang. "Look," their positioning seemed to say. "Look at the lovely young people we raised."

Essie shied away from the attention and, after the service, wanted to go home, but Eli, as a serving-man of the church, had to stay, and so Essie was resigned to help the matrons prepare lunch for the congregation.

In the process of getting downstairs to the kitchen, Essie was stopped a number of times to chat with this woman and that, hold this baby or that, and was asked countless questions about when she and Eli would have a baby or how she was enjoying married life. She answered politely, keeping her church smile on her face, determined not to put one toe out of line that would make Elias look unfavorable.

When it came to her step-father, however, she struggled. Holding her mother's arm possessively, Clayton approached his step-daughter and leaned down to kiss her cheek. Essie forced herself to stand still. She was quite proud of the fact that she did not run away screaming, but neither did she hug him back.

She stepped away from him as soon as was politely possible. "How are things going, Esmeralda?" Kyra asked fondly, trying to draw her daughter's attention away from her anger toward Clay.

"Great, Mama," Essie smiled. "Everything is going really well."

Essie saw the crew of serving members for the day starting toward downstairs and lifted the edge of her skirt a bit to move faster. She had to be down in the kitchens, quick, and stand with the rest of the ladies who made lunch, pretending that she had been of value.

Eli was asked to bless the meal and, after, was the first through the potluck line. He made a plate for Essie and met her by a table, handing it to her.

"Thank you!" she exclaimed. "I didn't expect that. It was really nice."

They sat down together and enjoyed a brief ten-minute pause when no one bothered them. Slowly, the rest of the congregation made it through the line and started to look for seats, and their lovely moment was ruined. Everyone wanted to talk to her husband and compliment him on his lovely work today and lovely wife. Several people even suggested that he should join the pastoral training program.

Finally, in a break of flowing people, Eli looked over and saw Essie cleaning up her dishes to bring them to the kitchen. He started, "Gem. Your plate is still a third of the way full."

"Yeah. That's the stuff I don't want to eat," she said, shrugging, nonplussed.

"But there's so much food left on it."

"Yes, and?"

Eli watched her go, horrified and once again aware of the antithesis of the worlds they grew up in.

Coming back to Eli from dropping her plate off in the kitchen, Essie was waylaid by Eli's mother.

"Esmeralda! Hello, darling, good to see you again," she stood on tiptoe, kissing the cheek of her much taller daughter-in-law.

"Hi, Mama Amy," Essie smiled and embraced the several younger children around her. "Are these all your grandchildren?"

Amy smiled and laughed. "All but one, darling. I had Eli, my oldest. Then his sister, Joanna, his brother Samuel, his next brother, Lucas, and then my next girl, Tabitha. These little ones are my grandbabies of those five all grown-ups and lucky for me close to home still," she said, scooping up a toddling little girl and holding her close to her heart. "Then with me at home, I still have the twins, Attarah and Adiel who are 17, Myra who's 16, and Sameera, 13."

"Nine babies!" Essie squealed.

Amy laughed again and shrugged, "We're fertile stock. Besides, the babies keep me young. You'll be having your own soon, I should think."

"Yes, I imagine so," she giggled. Although the idea of having more than one baby makes her heart sick with fear, Essie can see that whether or not it's the kids as she claims, something was keeping Mama Amy looking very young. Her reddish-brown hair had a few gray streaks and her face, though lined with laughter, shone smooth. Her mother-in-law pulled over a couple of older children and introduced them, "Esmeralda, these are my two youngest, Myra and Sameera." Both girls had their mother's light brown, almost red hair, as opposed to Eli's dark complexion.

"You met them at the wedding," Amy continued as the girls nodded politely and ran off to play once more. "And you'll meet the rest of them all at Richard's birthday party tomorrow."

"I look forward to it," Essie said amiably. "5 pm, right?"

"Six," Amy corrected.

"Oh. I could have sworn that Eli told me five," Essie laughed. "My bad."

"Maybe not. Goodness, that boy. He loves to be early," Amy laughed.

Essie filed the thought away as interesting.

That night she prepared for bed carefully. She wore a sheer pink nightgown that had been a shower gift from Kate. While Eli was in the bathroom brushing his teeth and getting ready to sleep, Essie situated herself on the edge of her bed brushing her hair. She felt like a siren as she did, preparing to bring down a man with a pretty body and voice.

Elias padded out of the bedroom sleepily, "Hey, gem, can I turn out the lights?" He turned and saw her and looked away. Eli took one glance and immediately turned off the lights. Essie exclaimed that she needed the light to finish getting ready, but Eli had to get himself together. Even though she was his wife, he felt sinful looking at her in that dress, body on display through the filmy cloth. The pink color made her cheeks appear flushed and pretty. He had seen in one glimpse that she was flawless. He had, of course, seen her like so before, but there was something different about seeing her so comfortably, provocatively strewn out on the bed doing as casual and mesmerizing a task as brushing her curly blond locks.

"Come here, Eli. And turn the light on, honestly," Essie exclaimed playfully. *Come hither, come hither.* Eli turned on the lights and came to sit behind her. She relinquished the brush and leaned back, sighing in pleasure as his hands and the bristles moved over her head. "Thank you, Eli. I really like that," she moved back into his lap, reclining against his chest. He fell for it all without a single negative thought. Essie noted with some embarrassment and some pride that she had managed to arouse him so fully.

Eli turned his head down and took her lips to his. His hands were on her little body, and he pulled her flush to him with a soft groan as he kissed her passionately. Expertly opening her mouth against his and moving with it in a way she had never experienced. His tongue touched hers tentatively, and she let out a sharp breath at the new motion. He pushed her back gently until she was lying on the bed, and he ran his hands over her willing body. Soft, mounded breasts, small waist, widening hips. He reveled in the beautiful creature that was his wife and thought how lucky he was and was glad that she had overcome her reluctance in the bedroom.

Lying in the wake of their love-making, Eli breathed in the scent of her, basking in the idea that they had their whole lives ahead of them and turned to go to sleep.

Essie was feeling completely different. How could his expressions of 'love' through physicality be true love if it was abused so easily? She had purposefully drawn him to her tonight to get him in a good mood before she approached him about something he would never want to talk about sober. Now, here he was, drunk off of fleshy things and soft. Manipulatable. He had rolled over, ready to sleep. She intended to get some answers. She rolled toward him and snuggled against his warm back. He was awake again as soon as her hands touched his bare skin. "Elias?" she murmured.

He turned over, capturing her in his arms and kissing her again. "What is it, gem?"

"Mama Amy told me that Papa Richard's birthday party starts at 5 pm tomorrow."

"Yep," he answered smoothly, kissing her forehead.

Essie pulled him closer to her, making sure she had his full attention. "Eli," she murmured, "You are the one who told me it started at 5. When I spoke to Mama Amy today she said 6."

He opened his mouth to respond, eyes alert and thinking hard.

Essie sealed his mouth with hers and then said, "And guess what she followed it up with? She said, 'goodness that boy loves to be early'. So do you know what time the thing starts at?"

Eli moved onto his side kissing her in what felt like a patronizing embrace. "Esmeralda, it starts at 6. Yes, I told you 5. Yes, I like to be early. Could you explain why you're so upset by that idea because I really don't understand?"

"It's the fact that you lied to me!" Essie exclaimed.

"For a good reason!"

"And what reason was that," she challenged.

"Uh… so we'd be on time."

"What's that supposed to mean?"

"Come on, gem…"

"No, answer!"

He rolled his eyes. "You take a really long time to get ready to go," he flopped onto his back lazily.

"So, instead of telling me what was wrong and that you were dissatisfied with my ability to get ready because I like to *look nice* before going out, you decided you'd just tell me that we had to be there an *hour early* so that we would… what!"

"Be on time?" Eli closes his eyes, trying to drift out of the way of her screeching.

"No! That's not acceptable! That's not going to work for me," Essie sat up on the bed, arms crossed and glaring.

Eli peeked one eye open and sighed, taking in her rigid posture, irritated scowl and all-around pert beauty. "Esmeralda, I'm sorry."

"You know, I'm starting to realize that I hardly know you," Essie said, blinking back tears.

"You think! You threw out an entire plate of food today!" Eli retorted, starting to get heated. "If I had done that when I was young, my daddy would have spanked me!"

"Your parents hit you!" Essie recoiled. "Oh, my god…"

"A spanking isn't the same as being beaten. I'm a firm believer in spanking kids."

"You'll never hit my baby. Ever!" Essie yelled.

"Your kid! They'll be *our* kids! And I will if they need it!"

"No child ever *needs* to be hit! And certainly not over a few mouthfuls of dinner left behind on the plate! You can't make people do everything you want, so you can't make a child do everything you want. Hitting them because they didn't finish their food… that's… that's just cruel!" Essie gasped.

Eli rolled his eyes again. "Esmeralda. It's a good thing you'll have me around because God knows your kids would run loose and have no rules whatsoever," she opened her mouth to retort angrily but he put a finger on her lips. "No, hear me out. You know why my father would have punished us if we wasted food like that? Because there were nine of us. Me and my eight little siblings. My mom was always pregnant and couldn't work so at the end of each month, with only one paycheck coming in, my mama and daddy had to make choices like buying food or paying rent. Of course, they couldn't afford fancy things and extras like private school and the newest clothing styles or even contraceptives. There was rarely enough for us to all eat until we were full and so when there was food, we ate happily and didn't care what it was because we were starving!"

"You're exaggerating," Essie pouted. "That doesn't happen anymore, it's the 21st century."

"Don't you call me a liar," Eli said seething quietly. "There was often so little food in the house that my parents would go hungry to feed us. My baby sister Sameera would cry because her tiny baby stomach was empty. She couldn't eat because my mother wasn't getting enough. I remember the night that my father called me and my brothers, Samuel and Lucas, downstairs to his office and told us that that night we were to leave the house and go see friends. There wasn't enough for us to have dinner, and we were men. We had to leave for a few hours because if my baby sisters saw that we weren't eating, they would insist on sharing, and then there wouldn't be enough for them. I was 19. Samuel was 14 and Lucas was 12. So if I ever dared throw out a plate of food, my father would beat me because that was food that could have gone to my siblings. He would beat me to protect his other children."

Essie was crying softly as Eli continued, "You grew up as an only child with one parent who doted on and spoiled you. You had a church, school, and iPhones and MacBook pros. You had Christmases that when you came downstairs in the morning, there was always a tree and piles of presents. You had a healthy mom. That's why you hate your step-father. He won't coddle you. Your mom paid for all of your tuition up until last month. I started working when I was eleven and put myself through law school. I went to the school closest to home so I could keep sending them checks so my little sisters could go on field trips and have birthday presents."

"So yes. We hardly know each other," he lowered his voice and wrapped his arms around himself as if hiding from the truth he had just set free in the room. "Esmeralda, I love you."

"Why didn't you tell me?" she sobbed.

He was silent in the darkness for a long moment. So long that Essie started to fear he wasn't even going to answer. Then he said, "I grew up so poor that I wore the same suit to church every single week for a year and washed it by hand. I also grew up in a family so proud that they would never ask for help. We struggled for a long time. And not once did my parents ask for anything. Then, after Sameera was off to primary school, Mama finally was able to get a job. With only half of the little ones still home, things got much better. So when I got out, the first thing I did was not forget that I was ever that destitute but build over it. I just didn't want you to know. And my parents wouldn't have wanted you to know."

"There's nothing wrong with asking people for things," Essie cried. "That's what the church is for! If your parents had asked…"

"My dad wanted us to learn that we could make it on our own."

"Eli…"

"I made it out, Esmeralda. They all did… And I learned independence and responsibility while I did. Not all of us have the lovely privilege of having everything handed to us on a literal silver platter. So don't you judge me or them. Don't you dare judge us," still rolling in anger, Eli turned over and tried to go to sleep but couldn't close his eyes with all that anger boiling between them.

Essie turned over and wept silently into her pillows. She couldn't imagine growing up that way. She was angry at him—furious that he had lied to her about what the start time of the event was. It seemed like such a small thing, but she was just so angry. So angry that she couldn't get past it.

Neither of them slept well that night.

Eli watched as Kate came down the aisle. All blue taffeta and cream. She looked like a princess, smiling and nodding to the many guests that had come to see his special day. On the arm of her copper-haired brother, they were a handsome pair and they smiled fondly at Eli as they split off to the sides.

Eli barely noticed his cousins. He was focused on the slim beauty that was standing in the doorway behind them. He watched as Essie smoothed the long white skirt of her

At the altar, Mama Kyra handed Essie off to Eli with a kiss on both of their cheeks, and the Minister stepped forward. He gave a speech about the beauties of marriage and read from the Bible. Eli's sisters—Joanna, Tabitha, Attarah, and Adiel—sang a gorgeous quartet piece. Tears flowed, and smiles shone through.

Eli didn't see any of that either. Before and after the ceremony, he thanked his sisters and the pastor but during the ceremony, he had eyes only for Essie. At Pastor James' suggestion, the two eagerly joined hands and repeated their vows.

Essie went first and broke down into happy tears. Eli wanted to take her into his arms right then and there but restrained himself, squeezing her fingers gently. Then he spoke and as he began, he started to understand why Essie cried. He too felt like sobbing as he repeated I take thee, Esmeralda, to my wedded wife, to have and to hold from this day forward, for better or for worse, for richer or for poorer, in sickness and in health, to love and to cherish, till death us do part, according to God's holy ordinance. *She was his. Until the good Lord saw fit to part them through death.*

Lying in his cold marriage bed, Eli suddenly reflected that from then until death was forever. And forever was a very long time.

"Essie?" Eli offered her his arm as he got out of the car and came around to open her door. She accepted the olive branch gratefully, not eager to look like a bickering couple in front of her mother, her new mother, and all Eli's siblings and friends.

Their fight from the previous night still unresolved; there was a notable coolness between the young couple. They didn't speak much to each other, and though she held his arm, Essie was not cuddling toward him as two embroidered wedding rings intertwined and as she once may have done.

"Eli! Eli's here!" A sudden shout from a petite redhead burst across the yard. She sprinted toward him, and the rest of the party followed. Essie recognized her as the youngest Darcy daughter, Sameera. She had been introduced to her yesterday at church, but, then, she had not been as perfectly thrilled as she was now. Her yellow dress fluttered, and red hair streamed behind her as she leaped into her beloved big brother's arms. The other siblings followed, and Eli was soon engulfed by them. One girl, looking most like Eli with the same dark hair and chocolate eyes hugged onto him, refusing to like go as if he were the prodigal son she hadn't seen in years. Even the brothers that Essie had heard much about hugged him.

She started to understand how much he had carried the family. He made it out and became a beacon of hope for the others. They too could make it. And they all had sent checks back to make the way smoother for the little ones.

Essie stepped out of the way and watched. One of Eli's brothers that she remembered blurrily from the wedding winked at her but other than that she hardly stood out at all. She wanted to run to her mom or Kate and tell them everything but her feet were rooted in place. She couldn't knock the thought of what would Eli say if he knew she ran to her mommy or best friend every time that her feelings were hurt. As independent as he was, he wouldn't be impressed.

She lifted her chin proudly. He might be a little bit older than she. Okay fine, several years older. But she could be as emotionally independent as he. If he didn't need to talk to anyone, she didn't either. She would figure it out on her own. Starting with forgiving him of her petty issues and moving on with her life. Loving him. Until death do them part.

Chapter 5

"And so without further ado… the graduating nurses of Greenfield Academy, 2016!"

Essie and her class jumped up, cheering. Essie and Kate squealed and hugged each other just as they had done four years earlier at their high school graduation.

Kate screamed something into Essie's ear, but she couldn't hear due to the blasting music and other people's shrieks around them. Essie realized that she was crying, tears of happiness. She felt a strange twisting in her stomach and smiled. Happy nerves. She had done it. She had graduated. She met eyes with Eli in the crowd and grabbing Kate's hand she dragged her friend toward Eli and Andy.

Mingling later among guests and students and teachers, Essie felt the twisting again. Stronger this time. It didn't hurt, but it didn't feel right. Essie made her way away from the throngs of people and leaned against a tree. It was getting to be winter, and she wished for Eli's coat. She decided that in a moment when she was feeling a bit better, she would go and get it. She stood up to take a step away from the tree, and she stumbled, landing on her hands and knees.

Kate was at her side immediately, waving off Eli, saying that it was probably woman issues, and leaving him standing with Andy helplessly. She knelt beside Essie. "Hey, you okay?"

"Yeah," Essie said. For some reason, she was having trouble catching her breath.

"Essie!" Kate exclaimed. "What's wrong with you?"

"Stop freaking out," Essie laughed breathlessly. "It's just, I feel a bit lightheaded."

"Why?" Kate demanded. "Have you felt like this before? What have you eaten today?"

"I've had a few moments like it before. I…" Essie frowned. "I fainted a couple of times this last month."

Kate shifted the way she was sitting. "Sorry, that time of the month."

Essie's frown deepened. "Are you on your period?" She demanded. "Don't we usually sync up?"

"Yeah…" Kate made a sudden curious face. "Essie, when *was* the last period you got?"

"Kate no… it's not that! I've had no other symptoms. I should have been throwing up and tired and stuff," Essie shook her head.

"When was your last one, Esmeralda."

"May," she admitted.

"Essie, don't you think it's possible that you might be pregnant? You've been having unprotected sex with the guy for almost six months," Kate said seriously.

Essie laughed. "No. Of course not. Kate, come on, I'm not pregnant!"

"Are you secretly on the pill?" Kate said completely serious.

"N-no… should I take a test?" Essie said uncertainly.

"No," Kate ruled. "Tomorrow morning, I'm taking you to the doctor's office."

Eli finally came over, unable to watch his cousin and wife sit in the dirt and having a serious conversation in hushed tones without knowing if everything was okay. By then, Kate was helping Essie to her feet and then smiled reassuringly at Eli and Andy. "Don't worry, perfectly fine," Kate breezed by, practically dragging Essie by the hand to the buffet tables.

"Hi, Esmeralda," Eli smiled over at her. "I was just talking to your professor here and one of his colleagues."

Eli extended a hand to her, and she went to him, feeling safe and comfortable under his arm. "Good afternoon, Professor Witney."

The professor smiled and shook her hand politely. "This is my good friend Dr. Chai. I was just talking to her about your amazing work in all of your classes."

Essie blushed and shook the doctor's hand saying charmingly, "I hope everything said was true, Professor."

"Of course, Mrs. Darcy. You've been an exceptional student. If you'll excuse me, I have to step away and speak to another student." The professor shook Essie and Eli's hands again and moved away.

Eli took a quick analysis of the situation and kissed Essie's cheek, "I'll talk to you later, gem. I'm going to see Kate."

Essie stood awkwardly as Eli left her standing with the doctor.

"Mrs. Darcy, first of all, congratulations on your graduation," Dr. Chai began politely.

Essie inclined her head. "Thank you, Ma'am."

"I'd like to offer you a job at the Newcastle Hospital," she continued.

Essie started. "Oh... I..."

"Don't feel the need to answer now. I wanted to ask you alone but I understand if you'd like to speak with your husband first about it before making a decision. It is a big decision. And I expect that you have received several other offers."

"I just didn't expect to have to choose so soon," Essie laughed.

"Think about it, dear. Have a good evening and congrats again," Dr. Chai bowed slightly to excuse herself.

Walking toward Kate and Andy, Elias was intercepted by Greg. The friend grabbed his arm, and Eli spun quickly exclaiming once he saw him, "What are you doing here?"

Greg blushed a bit. "I came to see Rachel. She just graduated."

"Rachel Gretel... our boss' assistant, Rachel?"

"Yep! Only not our boss' assistant anymore. She quit. She's going into nursing." There was a pause. "I mean... obviously."

Eli inwardly groaned. Stuck with Nyota. Oh, well, she would learn. The question was... how fast? "I didn't know you guys were so close." He commented to Greg, "That she'd invite you to her graduation."

Greg blushed again, "It happened quickly."

"Well, congrats," Eli laughed.

"Thanks. Hey, I actually came over to talk to you about something else," Greg continued.

"Okay?" Eli raised his eyebrows. "Shoot."

"Have you considered starting our own firm?"

Eli bit his lip. "I… I have. I think it's a really good idea…"

"But it's not the right time."

"It's not terrible timing actually…" Eli pondered. "With Esmeralda graduating, she'll start working and maybe now is an okay time?"

"Think about it. I really think we can do this."

"Okay. I'll think and I'll talk to Esmeralda."

"Essie? Come on! It's time for the game!"

Essie pulled her hair into a ponytail as she ran into the living room. "I'm here! I'm on time!"

"Two minutes late," Eli answered with a smirk, looking at his stopwatch.

"But you only had to call me once!" Essie looked at him brightly. "That's bonus marks for me."

"Whatever," Eli laughed, arranging himself to face her on the couch. She pulled herself together cross-legged in her silky pajamas and long blond ponytail, face framed with tendrils of gold curls.

"You go first," Essie offered.

Eli nodded and looked down at his cue cards. "Okay. So. How do you feel about having graduated?"

Essie stretched lazily and smiled at Eli. "Liberated! I feel so free."

"Happy?"

"Extremely," Essie giggled. "Next."

"Okay. What's your plan now?"

"I don't really have one," Essie shrugged.

Eli looked concerned and vaguely horrified. "You don't have any inkling of a plan whatsoever?"

"I mean… That's why we play the game, isn't it?" Essie pointed out.

The game. It was something they had started doing every night Monday through Friday just to ask each other questions and talk. Essie affectionately called it the dating game since most of the stuff they talked about were, in hindsight, topics they should have discussed *before* getting married. Some of the things were what Eli liked to call deal-changers. He didn't think that if he had known it before he had proposed he wouldn't have done it (they weren't deal-*breakers*), but they were things that he would have had a different outlook on what he was getting into.

"Yes, that's why we have the game," Eli sighed.

"So… I'll figure out a plan," Essie said nonchalantly.

"Your turn," Eli reposed, resigned.

"Okay. If I could have done one thing differently this last term, what would it have been?" Essie asked.

Eli thought through the lists. More affectionate, less emotional… he thought about the amazing dinner that she had prepared tonight even after her graduation ceremony. He loved having her home and around. He liked being the only one working and supporting her. He liked needing to be needed. "Be home more often," he answered.

Essie looked up in surprise. "Really?"

He nodded. "I like being Mr. Darcy. I like coming home to delicious meals and a clean house."

"I love doing that stuff for you," Essie smiled, thrilled that he noted and appreciated the work that she did around the house. She felt that that was the best way for her to let him know that she loved him, and she was glad that he was picking up on that.

"I also wish that you would say I love you more often," Eli continued.

Essie's eyebrows drew together. "Why?"

Eli jumped in surprise. "Why! I mean… it's nice to hear…"

Essie shrugged, "I guess, but words are just words. It doesn't mean anything."

"Esmeralda…"

Essie held up a hand. "Let me stop you there. We don't bicker during the game. It's against the rules."

"I wasn't going to…"

Essie raised her eyebrows like an irate primary teacher. "We have 25 minutes more. No bickering."

Eli graced her with a small smile. "Of course," he took his second turn asking, "How would you feel about me starting my own business?"

Essie clapped her hands without hesitation. "I think that's a wonderful idea!"

"Really?"

"Yes!"

"Okay then," Eli said in surprise. "I didn't expect you to be so excited about it. Can I ask… why?"

"You'll be home more often and have more flexibility and less stress!" Essie said cheerfully. "You'd have no commute so it'd be cheaper in the long run. I've heard that being self-employed is great."

"Umm… alright."

The game finished and further conversation about the I Love You words avoided; Eli reached to check his phone before climbing into bed with Essie for the night. "Gem… Mama Kyra called again. She wants you to call her back.

She said you haven't spoken to her except for church all month? Everything okay?" he asked in concern, cognizant of the close relationship the two had maintained for years.

Essie nodded her head, the only thing peeping out from under the blue duvet. "I just… haven't had the time."

"Okay," Eli answered doubtfully.

Under the blankets, Essie finalized the time for her appointment with the doctor and Kate for 1 pm. As Eli turned off the lights, Essie felt a strange sense of quickening again in her stomach. Hugging her arms around herself, she felt her stomach being harder, less fleshy and soft. She felt for a curve and found none. No. This was all a precaution. She wasn't pregnant. She couldn't be.

She thought about her mom again and reflected guiltily that she should probably call her back at some point. She had tried to distance herself a little bit, wanting to manage her emotional state and her relationship with Eli on her own for a while, but if—God forbid—she was pregnant, she would have to reach out. And of course, she would want to.

Essie woke up at 4:30 am and felt terrible. She tossed and turned for a while, exhausted but sleepless. She couldn't pinpoint why she was so uncomfortable. She just felt that nothing felt right anymore. Lying on her side was uncomfortable; her back was worse; and her stomach was the worst.

Eventually, her tumbling woke Eli, and he reached over sleepily, mumble asking if she were alright and drawing her toward him. Essie murmured back something about being fine, and Eli dozed back off. Essie lay awake. She felt too close to him and squirmed away only to have his half-asleep grip tighten on her as she tried to escape.

It was too early to get out of bed, but Essie couldn't sleep. She dozed and dreamed fitfully until she saw the clock strike 6, and then, without waking Eli, she slid out of bed and padded into the kitchen. She put the kettle on, thinking to herself, "this day needs tea." She was reminded of Kyra as she did. Cradling the hot mug, she sat at the kitchen table with her laptop open in front of her and put on her favorite TV series. She watched four episodes and the sunrise before she started to nod off, fueled by a lack of sleep and anxiety for the afternoon's meeting.

Eli found her at 8 am, face down on her keyboard, show still playing. Expression soft as he moved the computer away from her and kissed her forehead, he lifted his exhausted wife and carried her back to bed where she stayed until lunchtime. He stayed home from work and wondered if she was okay. It didn't make sense to him that she would get up so early and then fall asleep on the table unless she was trying to escape him. There was something wrong with her. She was acting almost sick as if she didn't quite realize what she was doing. He wanted to be home when she woke up.

When she got out of bed for the second time, it was with a shriek and hardly a care for seeing Eli there. He watched helplessly as she leaped out of bed, rushed through the shower, and kissed him half-heartedly calling, "Love you, I'll be home for dinner, I'm going out with Kate!" over her shoulder.

Eli felt a rift of frustration opening up. He had learned that she expressed her love through actions and had tried to be there for her when she woke up by staying home from work. Instead of being grateful and realizing that he was trying to speak her love language, she was curt and flippantly used his as she rushed away.

Kate held her friend's hand as she sat in the waiting room. She led her through to the doctor's office and squeezed her fingers through the examination. Essie asked her to leave once she dropped her off at home. Essie saw Kate's face fall and hurried to reassure her that she would call her later and talk, but she wanted to be alone right now. Kate left respectfully, kissing Essie on the cheek and making her promise to take care of herself. Essie left, promise ungiven.

Inside the house, she was glad that Eli had left. All she felt like doing was going to bed. She knew that she shouldn't, but she didn't want to do anything. Home alone, she got a huge bowl of ice cream and carried it into the bedroom, climbing back into bed and balancing both the frozen bowl and her computer on her stomach. She quickly moved them, thinking twice about the wisdom of that and putting them both beside her as she rolled onto her side. She opened her email and carefully worded her graceful refusal to Dr. Chai's offer. And then copied and pasted the declination letter to the address of every other doctor and institution that had made her an offer.

Essie lay on her side, and then she felt something inside of her move. Her hands flew to her abdomen in a protective gesture she hadn't been making two days ago. But then… two days ago, she hadn't known as much as she did now. She didn't know if she should feel happy or sad or angry or scared or any other emotion. She felt them all as she felt the movement again. She was crying as she put her hands on her belly and whispered, "Hello, baby."

Settling in at the office and putting his feet up, Eli pulled out his phone. His friend and partner answered on the first ring. "Hey, Greg. It's me, Elias."

"Eli! Nice of you to call. I'm actually in a conference meeting with Mrs. Grail right now."

"Oh," Eli answered. He couldn't help but wonder why he had picked up his call. Elias himself felt embarrassed to be on the phone with Greg while he was in a conference meeting. It just seemed rude.

"Don't worry, I just had a good feeling about why you called. Is it what I thought it was?"

"I think so. I'm in. I'm interested in leaving BlueCo for the new firm. Esmeralda was actually… really excited about it," Eli smiled into the phone, puzzled.

"I like this wife of yours more and more. I'll have to meet her someday," Greg joked. "Well, great. I'll have my assistant print off all the papers for you and we'll be green-lighted by the end of the day."

"Okay… great," Eli said. Greg had already hung up.

Eli walked in the door, expecting to hear Essie's cheerful voice welcoming him back or the smell of dinner on the stove. The foyer was cold and empty. The house was silent. "Esmeralda?" he called. There was no answer.

He walked upstairs wondering if she was still out with Kate and had lost track of time as she so often did. He saw her, back in bed, tears dried on her cheeks and a bowl half-full of melted ice cream on the side table. "Oh, gem…" he murmured. He didn't know what was wrong with her these days. Something wasn't right. He wasn't sure whether or not to wake her. He figured it would be kinder to go and cook dinner and let her wake up on her own terms but as he stood to get up, a little hand reached for his and pulled him back down.

"Hey, Eli," she whispered tiredly.

"Esmeralda, everything okay?" he asked, clearly concerned.

"Can you grab my purse from the corner? There's a blue envelope in it that I want you to see," she said sleepily. Waking up, Essie sat up and leaned against Elias. She wanted to be as close to him as she could. The few times that she did, however, were the few times that he didn't seem to notice or want her there. She took his arm and draped it around her. Eli looked surprised and then pleased, pulling her close.

He held the blue envelope out to her, but she shook her head. "You open it."

Elias peeled back the flap and drew out a little black and white image. His eyes widened. "What is it…"

"It's an ultrasound picture, Eli," Essie answered softly.

"Esmeralda is that… is it…"

Essie nodded. "It's mine. Ours, I guess."

His eyes shone with tears, and he jumped off the bed, pulling her with him and dancing her in a circle across the room. "You're pregnant!"

Essie giggled and nodded. "Yes, Eli."

"You're going to have a baby!"

"Yes!"

"When did you find out?" he demanded, sweeping her into his arms and kissing her soundly. "Oh, my God, I can't believe it! I'm so happy!"

She pulled away, laughing, even as exhausted as she was. "I found out this morning. I went to the clinic with Kate."

"That's what you were in a hurry for," he exclaimed, suddenly feeling bad for being frustrated. "Did you know?"

"No, I had no clue. It's Kate who suggested it. She saw that I was feeling faint and discovered that I had missed my period for several months."

"You didn't seem to have many signs," Eli acclaimed again.

"I know, Elias."

"How far along are you?"

"Twenty-one weeks," she said faintly.

"Twenty-one weeks! And you didn't know!"

"Yes, Elias."

"No nausea or exhaustion until now."

"I know, Eli. That's why I didn't think anything of it."

He knelt in front of her to cup her stomach in his hands and kiss all over it, whispering to the baby, "Hi honey, it's daddy. I'm really excited to meet you. And I love you."

Essie watched him, relaxing and starting to feel excited. She had a baby inside of her. She didn't feel connected to it at all. Shouldn't she feel motherly and protective or something? She wanted to bring it up with Eli but couldn't figure out how. She was happy because he was so happy.

"Does anyone else know?"

"No, just Kate."

"Can we go over and see my parents tomorrow? Or would you rather tell Mama Kyra first? Or is there someone else?"

"I'd like to tell them all at once," Essie said. This was the one thing that she had really made up her mind on. "I don't want anyone to think we're playing favorites with the sides of the family."

"My beautiful wise Esmeralda," he stood up, and she went into his arms, needing to feel his support. Her arms twined around his neck and his firm around her waist as if they were about to slow dance. He held her and kissed the top of her head, and Essie started to cry.

Astonished, Eli pulled back from her. "Esmeralda!"

She shook her head, unable to speak through the tears.

He pulled her off of her feet and sat her on his lap. "Gem, tell me."

"Eli, I…" she let out a sob and caught her breath before continuing. "I… I don't feel anything. I'm not excited. I want to be excited. I should be!"

"You're just shocked," Eli soothed. "Excitement will come. I promise."

"We'll be good parents, right?" Essie begged.

"Of course."

"Promise, Eli?"

"Of course."

"Am I too young to be having a baby?"

"Of course not!" he exclaimed. "You're the perfect age. And you have me. I know what to do. You forget that I was present for 9 of my mother's pregnancies. I'll take care of you," he cradled her, kissed her forehead, and murmured to her, rocking her back and forth.

"Okay."

"Okay? I promise, everything will be fine."

"Okay."

"I'm going to make dinner. You just stay here."

Essie wriggled out of his arms. "No! No, please, I can do it."

Eli looked at her curiously. "Are you sure? You're feeling well enough?"

"Yes. I want to. I love cooking."

"My little housewife," he laughed.

"That's right," Essie giggled, glowing inside and out. She was his little housewife.

Essie rang a little bell as she threw open the door to the dining room. "Le diner est servis," she gave a little curtsy, having taken off her apron and changed into one of her evening gowns.

"French and the dining room instead of the kitchen!" Eli gasped, coming over from watching TV on the couch.

"It's a special day," Essie giggled. The dress was cinched tight around the waist, and the rounding curve of her stomach could be seen.

He couldn't help himself and took her in his arms, twirling her around the room.

"Eli!" she cried out, reaching to smooth down her hair, but she was laughing and he didn't stop.

"I just want to dance, princess," he laughed.

"Sit down," she said mock sternly.

"Okay, okay."

The meal that she served took the better part of three hours to prepare and while it was delicious, it was the physical display of the dishes that caught Eli off guard. Everything was plated beautifully, drizzled, dipped, and dusted. Seasonings were sprinkled around, and sprigs of herbs were slipped artfully into the array.

"Esmeralda, it's beautiful."

She lifted her head proudly. "Thank you."

"Would you ever consider hosting an event for some of my work friends? I think you would do so well."

"That's my job, isn't it? Your lovely housewife and hostess? A job I absolutely love," she giggled.

"You are perfect," Eli smiled. She was. She was everything that he could ever have wanted in a wife. He vaguely remembered a dinner that Essie and he had attended with Kate and Andy and some mutual friends a few years ago. It was hosted by a rather conservative, old-fashioned couple, and while the men sat in one living room and watched TV, the women retired to another more sophisticated and elegant sitting room. When they came together for the meal, it became clear that the wife was only hosting the event because she and her husband thought it would be appropriate. She served with a frown, and while she wasn't downright rude to the guests, she wasn't friendly either.

Essie was perfect. She served with elegance and grace and a smile. Eli knew that she would never do anything to embarrass him or herself. She was perfect.

"Eli, I have some news for you. I think you'll like it," she still had the glow around her that Eli loved. She was beautiful and hardworking. He was sure that he would in fact love her news for him.

"Tell me."

"I turned down all of my offers to be a nurse. So that I can be home full time for you and our baby," she was still smiling, without knowing that her words changed everything.

Irrelevantly, Eli thought, *her words don't change everything, her actions do. But either way, everything has changed and it's a disaster.* He was still smiling too. "What do you mean?"

She looked at him, smiling, "I turned down the offers. Now I can be home and a mother and a wife." The smile faltered. "A-aren't you happy?"

Eli buried his face in his hands. "Esmeralda, today I quit BlueCo to start my own business. That's going to be expensive! One of us needs to be working!"

Essie stared at him. "Eli, what do you mean? You don't have a job!"

He rubbed his forehead, fighting irritation. If only she had told him about this! All his contracts with the company were already set in stone! There was no changing them, and to be frank, he didn't really want to! He wanted his own business. He shouldn't have to give up that dream for her, if only she could have told him about her plans before doing them!

Essie felt her heart start to sink. It was an expression she had heard many times throughout her life, but she felt it. A hard lump of dread sank into her belly like lead. All her plans... The ideas of dinners to host and parties to plan. The baby being born into designer onesies and name-brand shoes. He wasn't working, and she wasn't working which meant that there was no more money coming in. Why hadn't he told her about his plans? He had told her that he wanted her home more!

"Can you take back your refusals?" Eli demanded.

Essie nearly broke into frustrated tears but channeled all of the emotions into anger. Anger at him. "No, I can't, they've already been given away. Kate told me. Besides! Why should I? You promised you'd take care of me? You said over and over again that you would be the breadwinner, and you wanted me here at home and hosting and cooking and cleaning! That's my role! You were supposed to support us! Can't you take back your job?"

Eli stared at the little thing in front of him, uncomfortable, with child, and angry. He sat up straighter. Well, he was angry too! "Maybe I did, that's what you wanted to hear, right? But there was no reason that you couldn't have worked too while I pursued some of my dreams! What about me?"

"What about me?" Essie retorted. "I have dreams too! I thought I was coming into this to be a housewife and a mother! Don't my dreams count for anything?"

They sat, staring angrily at each other across the dining room table silently. Neither of them willing to back down.

"So where do we go from here?" Eli finally said, willing to put it behind and move forward. He was, after all, a grown-up adult and should be able to control himself. He was ready and willing to admit that they should have talked more about their plans but only if she would. He wouldn't take all of the steps; she should meet him in the middle, man of the house or no.

Essie knew that she couldn't give in. She gave in far too often. So often that he had obviously started thinking that she was so easy-going that he didn't need to discuss plans with her, and she would just give in. Just like that. And it was a no. No way. She wasn't going to. He had promised to take care of her. He was Mr. Darcy, a knight in shining armor! He was supposed to be everything that she had wanted since she was a little girl dreaming about princesses and fairy tales. This new life was supposed to be her fairy tale, and he was doing it all wrong!

"Esmeralda?"

She didn't answer him. She stared him down without saying a word. Dinner grew cold on their plates, and she started to get more and more uncomfortable and her lower back started to ache.

Neither one of them moved for ten minutes. Then half an hour. Then the clock ticked that an hour had passed. Neither of them would cave in. Essie pushed her dishes away from her and laid her head down on the table and quickly fell asleep.

Only when he was sure that she was no longer awake did Eli stir to move her to bed. He knew that it was ridiculous, and she would know he had moved her when she woke up in the bed tomorrow morning but he refused to sacrifice his pride. He picked her up and kissed her belly softly. He hadn't forgotten that she was carrying his baby. He felt bad that he had caused her so much stress while she was pregnant. And the day she found out, too. That was a lot of stress.

He tucked her into the bed and kissed her forehead. She didn't even stir. Eli went back to the kitchen to wash the dishes. He looked regretfully at the beautiful plates that she had prepared and carefully set the dessert away in the fridge. It would keep until tomorrow. She would be talking to him by then.

As he cleaned up, he thought back through all of their conversations. Had he encouraged her to quit her job options? Maybe he had. He remembered commenting that he liked having her at home. And of course, he had said a few times that he would take care of her. He wanted to be able to take care of her. He should be able to take care of her. That's what a husband does. Was she, maybe, right to be mad at him? The more he thought about it, the more he was confused and scared. What if they couldn't come back from this argument? What if this was the end of Mr. and Mrs. Darcy? He didn't know what he would do. He loved her. He wanted to be her knight. But what if he wasn't enough?

He tried to calm his fears. It would be fine. It was just a squabble. They would get through it.

Essie woke up the next morning. She saw Eli smiling slightly in his sleep, handsome and sweet. For a moment she couldn't remember anything of what they had been arguing. And then it came back in a wave, and she rolled over to face away from him. She could win this. She could make everything go back to normal. He'd get a job again when he was tired of her being angry at him. She knew he would. He doted on her and hated seeing her upset. He would fix this. Everything would go back to how it should be. She closed her eyes again, pretending to sleep. He would fix this. And she would sleep in. She had a baby to grow, after all.

Chapter 6

Eli was very careful to be as wonderful as possible. He served the fancy dessert the next day, but she pushed it away, saying that she wasn't hungry. For the rest of the week, Esmeralda stayed in bed and claimed that she was tired and in pain. Eli wanted to call her out for faking, but he wasn't actually sure. It could be that she really was suffering, and he would feel like an absolute zounderkite for being rude to her in that case. But she overplayed it. By the fifth day, he knew that there was nothing wrong with her other than a spiteful heart. Still, he played along, wanting her to come crawling back to him.

He bought and cooked her favorite foods. He washed dishes and did laundry. Eli brought home flowers and little gifts like new dresses and things for the nursery. She hardly responded. Eli felt like he was arguing with his little sister, Tabitha. Essie and his sister were nearly the same age, and he could remember fighting with her when they were kids. Everything he did was met with either contempt or disregard.

At some points, Elias almost felt like he was living with his little sister. She was acting so young! So childishly. He loved her, of course, but he felt no urge for any kind of romantic love or sexual love. At least, not toward her. He never ever even considered committing adultery but he was frustrated. That was the only word to describe it. Frustrated.

Church morning came, and he had to wonder whether or not she would join forces with him for church. He couldn't imagine how horrible it would be to have her push him to the lions at church and put their crumbling marriage out in public.

Essie knew that she couldn't do that. It would be embarrassing and rude not only to Elias and herself but also to her mother and her parents-in-law and all of Eli's brothers and sisters. Clayton would have a field day. No, that wouldn't happen. So she steamed her dark-green velveteen and brushed her hair. She put on her heeled boots and pinned on a black trilby with a forest green satin bow. She put on black gloves, painted on a pink church smile, and took Eli's relieved offered arm.

"Ready?" he asked as if they were walking into battle.

I suppose, Essie thought, *we are.* "Yes," she answered simply.

Eli was relieved that they made a good showing of a united front. No one suspected anything. It went even better than he had anticipated. He had been asked to serve again that day, and he did so elegantly. Essie made him look even better, helping out with the children's church and the potluck lunch afterward. She held his arm and said all the right things to all the right people. And of course, she was beautiful. He, in return, didn't comment when she overfilled her plate in front of him and discarded most of it. He defended her to Clay and spent lunch with Kyra as if nothing were wrong.

That night, he was rewarded with smiles and a few quiet, kind words in private. She let him touch the baby bump and kiss it. That night she let him make love to her. And that night, once she was asleep, Eli got up, grabbed a blanket from the pile of spares in the cupboard, and moved to the couch. He was radiating anger and couldn't stay in the bed with her while she slept so smugly.

The problem was that she was allowing him to do things, and he hated it. He stepped out of line; she didn't speak to him. He brought home roses three days in a row and acted as a shield to stepfather, and she would allow him to have things that were his right. He was tired of feeling like a dog in need of training. He didn't need anyone to train him with rewards and punishments. It wasn't fair, and it wasn't right. If he ever dared try that with her, she'd be home with her mama in a flash. He would have to let her. Everyone would. She was young and female and pregnant for the first time, people would say. They would say that she just needed her mother's support. Eli, of course, could definitely not go running to his mother. *He* was a grown man. *He* should be in charge of himself. *He* shouldn't be going running to his mom.

He spent the night tossing and turning until it was finally time to get up. In their bedroom, nestled among the quilts and pillows, Essie lay glowing and warm. She wouldn't be up until noon if Eli knew her at all. Nothing was fair.

"Greg wants to help us finish the basement," Eli started up casually as they ate breakfast one morning.

"Why would we let Greg help with that?" Essie answered just as politely. "That was for us to do. It was going to be an us project."

"Because once it's done, he would like to have a room down there as office space for our new firm."

"No," Essie continued nonchalantly.

"I think it's a good idea," Eli countered coolly. "Then I could be home more often."

Essie bit back the words forming on her tongue. *Your job isn't to be home. It's to work and support me and our baby.* Saying it would only lead to more of a mess. As it was, the conversation was hostile but tame. Those sentences would make it hostile and loud.

"I think it would be nice of him to help. And I think having an office here is ingenious."

"What if I say no?"

Eli made a face at her. He knew that she could be stubborn, but she was growing to learn that he could be too. If neither of them gave in, it would be a bloodbath. One that they had seen before and didn't like. But on this, Eli would get his way. Essie knew that. He had his heart and mindset, and it would be better to choose her battles and leave this one unchosen.

"Go ahead," Essie agreed. "It could be good."

"While we're making plans," Eli got up, carrying his dishes to the sink with a lackadaisical smirk, "My mom wants to know if we'll host Christmas this year."

Essie's hands suddenly shook so hard that she was afraid she would drop her mug. "Host Christmas? For the whole family! All your brothers and sisters and their spouses and children?"

"All my cousins too," Eli added offhandedly. "Fortunately, they consist of Andy and Kate, maybe Alec if Auntie Phoebe can be convinced to let him come."

"That's a lot of people," Essie met his challenging gaze head-on. "Can we afford it?"

Eli despised that question while Essie adored it. She asked it often, always wanting to point out that he was in the wrong and he should feel bad that she couldn't have everything that she wanted.

"It will be if we are frugal and careful with our finances and don't try to plan it too fancy," he shot back in as affable a tone as she had asked.

"Christmas isn't a time for parsimoniousness, love," Essie said, amiable but with a touch of sarcasm. "It's a time for liberation and generosity... I could ask my mama for a loan..." Essie taunted.

Eli's biceps grew taut. "That won't be necessary. We can handle it."

"Okay," Essie sing-songed.

Eli came over to her, and she lifted her chin to receive his kiss. He bent and kissed her belly before standing, *towering* over her and brushing his lips across hers. "Have a good day, darling. I love you."

Essie walked him to the door and smiled up at him. "I love you too."

As Eli walked out the door and drove off to work, they had the dual thought of, *but how long will simply love be enough?*

Essie found that she actually hated staying home. There was only so much cleaning to be done in a house the size of theirs. She found herself with lots of time to sit around and do nothing. She started baking. As one of their wedding gifts, they had been gifted with a cookie jar shaped like a Mother Hubbard Swan. As gruesome as Eli always joked it was, he had no issue with happily pulling off the head and having it be full of cookies. Essie filled it with a new recipe every Tuesday and Friday, but still, there was only so much baking she could do.

She got terribly tired of doing laundry and actually found herself missing her homework. She started reading often and writing personal little book reports on some of the stories. She discovered that often, she would choose that work over the housework that needed to be done.

Her mother and other women that she spoke to suggested that she take up arts and crafts. Those brief experiences taught Essie that she couldn't embroider or cross-stitch to save her life and she detested knitting. By Mama Amy's patient side, she completed one lumpy baby's sock and then retired gracefully from the sport.

One day, she spent three straight hours lying in front of the TV. She started daydreaming and then really dreaming.

Essie woke up, and all the walls around her were made out of floral printed fabric. She crawled around and around until she was dizzy and lost. She heard a voice calling her and calling her. It was her mother. Her mama was calling her but no matter how far Essie crawled, she couldn't get to her. She had created a labyrinth of tunnels in a giant fort all over the house. She couldn't find her way out but in the center, when she got there, she found huge bowls of popcorn and mugs of hot chocolate with marshmallows and cake. So much cake. She lay there and drifted off until she slept her way back to reality.

Essie blinked several times. She started to smile as she looked around the living room and saw all the potential for a house covering fort. She stood up and got to work.

Eli pulled into the driveway at the same time as always. The little house looked the same as it always did, and the suburban neighborhood looked consistent. He walked up the front steps to the house, not knowing what would be inside but knowing that whatever was, the biggest variable was the woman. She was the game changer. He never knew what kind of mood she would be in.

He opened the door and was met with the grave mouth of a tunnel. He dropped his computer bag in shock. "Esmeralda!"

"Come in and shut the door!" her voice came faintly from somewhere over the house.

He stepped inside, and immediately the entrance roof shrunk so that he would have to crawl. He set his bag to the side, wondering at how long this thing would have taken to set up and wondering if she had gotten any chores at all done that day. The whole place smelled like fresh baked goods.

"Esmeralda!"

"I'm going to stop answering. You're listening to where my voice is and that's cheating!" she giggled.

Eli shook his head as he started to crawl. It was ridiculous. Really perfectly ridiculous. Here he was, a grown-up man, crawling on his hands and knees like a child. Heading toward… where? He had no clue.

He had to admit that the tunnels were expertly crafted by someone who had to know what they were doing. The blankets weren't draped like a child would, over tables and chairs and dipping in the middle. They were stretched tight and secured to all of the furniture, be they walls or bookshelves or the couch. Eli scooted through the maze, finding a dead end near the living room somewhere and another through the kitchen. He found a clue under the dining room table that told him to look where he rarely had his eyes open. He started heading toward the bedroom, not only because the clue made sense but also because he had already explored most of the first floor.

Turning his head around the last corner, suddenly music started to play, and Essie popped out from under the bed. "Surprise!"

She climbed out and kissed his astonished cheeks. "What do you think? Isn't it marvelous?"

"It's something," Eli laughed. "It's rather… Esmeralda-ish."

"Why, thank you," she laughed. "Ooh! Look, I have snacks!" Wrapped in a huge blanket, Essie pulled out snacks and her laptop hooked up to two small speakers.

"Esmeralda, shouldn't we be doing actual work?"

"I figured you needed a break. Just to kick back and relax," Essie offered. "It's been… a strenuous few weeks."

"That's a good description." He nodded.

"I have the Princess Bride set up." Essie nudged.

"Who can say no to the princess bride," Eli joked. "The mere thought is… *inconceivable*," he winked.

Essie burst into laughter.

She had brought into the labyrinth every pillow they owned and arranged them for them to lie down on like reclining sultanas. He sat back, plumping the pillows behind her, and Essie leaned on his chest.

He was honestly surprised by her forwardness but appreciated it. She was different today. Maybe just lonely but either way, happy to have him. And he was happy to have her. Little and round and clinging to him. Loving him. He held her close, vowing to enjoy these moments whenever they came.

"Eli! I need you!" Essie called frantically.

Eli sighed and left his half-finished project in the basement and came up, brushing off sawdust. Essie was standing in their bedroom, hands holding long blond hair off of her neck and back. "I can't zip it up," Essie exclaimed, holding the back together with her other hand. "Help?"

Eli brushed his hands off, knowing that if he got dust and dirt on her dress, she would have his head. He tugged at the zipper and then pulled on it again. "It's stuck, Esmeralda."

"No, it'll go up," she gasped, sucking in her gut. "Try now."

"Gem, it's not going to go up. You need a maternity dress."

"I don't! My old clothes still fit!"

"This one doesn't."

"Are you calling me fat?"

"Esmeralda! You're six months pregnant!"

Essie turned and looked in the mirror, relaxing her breath. Her bump wasn't sticking out much, but she was considerably bigger than the size double zero tight fitting dress. "But that's my Christmas dress!" she spun around and glared at Eli. "Your guests will be here in nearly an hour. Why aren't you dressed yet! And what am I going to wear?"

Eli hugged her from behind, his hands resting on her bump and his cheek lying on her head. "It'll be okay. You don't need to stress about it. It's just our families coming."

Essie pulled away. "I'm not stressed."

"Okay, Esmeralda."

"I'm not!" she pushed him away. "Go get dressed. And shower!"

"One last thing, gem. You didn't think to try on the dress before now? Maybe you should have had a backup plan," Eli suggested. "Maybe you should have bought a new one."

Essie stopped moving toward the closet and looked at him sharply. "Excuse me?"

Eli froze. "I'm just saying… I think that this could have been avoided."

Essie took several quick icy little steps toward him and glared nearly a foot up at him. Her small height didn't make her any less terrifying as her gaze shot daggers at him. "I don't think we could *afford* a new dress at the moment," she hissed and stomped away.

Eli flopped onto his back on the bed. Now he'd done it. She wasn't wrong. He had spoken before thinking. But still, he doesn't appreciate the jab at the fact that they hadn't been doing well. They had started to be very, very careful with money; there was little leftover for fripperies. There was nothing left over for a new dress or any maternity clothes.

Seething, Essie stormed into the closet, throwing clothes off of hangers and digging through drawers. She was looking for a dress that would be appropriate, but all she could see was a blur. She blinked the moisture out of her eyes. She wouldn't—she couldn't cry. She was going to make this day spectacular if it killed her. And she would do it on the stupid budget that Eli had set out. She had never felt so poor, and she hated it. Eli was fine with it, but he had grown up poor.

At least he tried to present that way. Eli dressed in an old suit, trying to force his mirror reflection to smile. He was fine with wearing an old suit. He remembered the years as a child when he would wear the same two outfits every day, not because he loved them, but because he had no other choice. He tried to convince himself that he was fine with living this way because he grew up this way but in truth, the fact that he grew up this way made it worse. This was everything that he had worked to escape for the last 20 years of his life. He had wanted out. He had worked his ass off to get out, and now he was back. Essie should be able to have a new dress every day if she wanted. Eli wished that she was working but with the other part of his mind, knew that he would feel terrible if she was working and he wasn't.

When the door first rang, Essie was comfortably dressed in an old, burgundy dress. It was still in good condition, and the piece clung softly over her curves, long-sleeved and falling smoothly to the ground with a sequined hem. She felt old and lumpy.

The first people to arrive were Joanna and her family. Eli's sister kissed Essie's cheek friendly and polite and oohed and awed over her pretty dress and the growing baby bump.

"Come on in!" Essie exclaimed, showing them into the living room.

"Thank you," Joanna looked smiling around the foyer and front of the house. "It's beautiful. I love what you've done with the decoration."

Essie started to feel better. The house was her pride and joy. She loved it and had loved working on it. "Thank you," she hugged her sister-in-law.

"I'm so sorry, again, that I wasn't able to make it to your wedding," Joanna begged pardon. "You know that we live pretty far away but I wish that I could have made it for my big brother and new baby sister."

"Thank you. Can I get you tea? Or for… your husband? We have some snacks prepared but I wasn't going to put them out until others arrived…" Essie fretted.

Joanna put a steadying hand on her shoulder, "Let me help you. I know we're a bit early, the least we can do is help." She helped one of the little ones milling about her feet get their coat off and handed him off to the husband. "By the way, I don't believe you've met my husband, Gavin, and our sons, Tariq and Jason."

"A pleasure to meet you all," Essie smiled at the little ones and offered Gavin a one-armed hug.

"So, do you know the sex of your baby yet?" Joanna asked as she followed Essie into the kitchen.

"Not yet. Eli wanted to wait until the birth of the baby. He wants a surprise," Essie rolled her eyes. She suddenly looked up, shocked at how she was acting, and to his own sister too! How would she take it?

Joanna laughed. "Sounds like Eli."

Suddenly, Essie was curious. "Were you close with Eli growing up?"

Joanna looked thoughtful as she hulled berries for a fruit platter. "We were closest in age, yes… and united in some issues—I guess Eli has told you that our family wasn't the best off when we were young?"

Essie nodded for her to go on.

"So, we were united in that but we were never super close. I adored him, and he loved me just as much but I'm not his favorite."

"Who's his favorite?"

"Tabitha," Joanna laughed without hesitation. "Tabitha and the rest of our little sisters. Eli is 14 years older than her, and they were inseparable. Tabby is the one who looks most like him, same dark hair and general dark features. The rest of us are varying shades of redhead, like mom."

"I'm sorry," Essie bowed her head apologetically.

"Why?"

"For… all of that. It doesn't seem right that he would have favorites… or that you'd be the only one left out of that group of favorites."

"It's not like that. I'm no Tabby, but still, we're good friends, and I have the other boys. Lucas and Sam."

"Why the other little girls and not you?"

"Because I was never a little girl like they were. I grew up fast. Faster than he could keep up with. The others are young, and he likes to protect them and feel like they need him. I never needed him like that. Elias needs to feel needed," Joanna looked her over with a knowing smile. "You're not much older than Tabitha."

"But I'm not a sister, I'm a wife."

"I don't think that in a lot of things, it makes a difference," Joanna hums. "How has it been working out for you, having him be so much older than you and want to take on that brotherly protective role?"

"It's not like that!" Essie said quickly. "It's all quite fine. Could you take that plate out to the living room? I think I can hear more guests arriving."

"Of course," Joanna answered smoothly. "You call me if you ever want to talk and tell me the truth, MmKay?"

Essie watched in astonishment as her sister-in-law, she was sure she would never understand, swept out of the room with a wink. But then again… whatever that was, it was clear that she had an ally.

The house was full of laughing children and the joy of Christmas. Music played, and games were sprawled over the living room floor. Eli's brothers and Andy and Kate were down in the basement, admiring the work going on there. Essie was chatting with his brother's wives, and Joanna while helping control the little ones who suddenly seemed to be twice as many with double the number of legs for running and sticky hands for trailing over the walls. Essie was fretting since she didn't think dinner would hold, but there was still a large group coming. Eli's parents and younger siblings were not yet there. All in all, Eli thought everything was going great.

There was a knock on the door, and the older children swarmed around it, eager to see who was there. Essie breathed a sigh of relief as Eli opened the door and let in their last guests. As soon as they came in and had their coats and hats off and wraps were carried off and left in the guest room, the dining room doors were thrown open. The whole family, laughing and chatting made their way over to the buffet-style meal and things started to relax.

Eli was thrilled to see all of his family in one place once again. He loved Christmas. He had always loved Christmas because his parents had always made it work, no matter how they had to.

Only one person was more thrilled to see him than he was to see them. Tabitha watched with distaste as her beloved older brother played left hand to the new wife. She knew she was supposed to cherish Esmeralda as a sister and love her as such, but she just couldn't. She was sure that she would have been able to have they met as friends, but she was the girl who had stolen her brother away. She could never love her.

Tabitha took pleasure in the fact that Eli made a plate of food for her and not for Essie. He came over, and Tabitha graced him with her most charming smile, and he hugged her with his free arm, kissing the top of her head. He offered her his arm, and they went off to find a quiet place to talk and catch up.

Tabitha caught the disapproving glance of her mother and Joanna who thought she was her mother. Even Essie herself made a face as she saw the two disappearing. Finally, in a quiet space, Tabitha blurted out, "How can you stand it? Living with that witch. She so spoiled and rude… not to mention she doesn't appreciate you at all!"

Eli shook his head reprovingly at his brash little sister, "Tabby, I love her. I thought you did too."

"I did. Before you married her," Tabitha wrinkled her nose. "I don't know what you see in her."

"Wait until you're married," Eli said knowingly with all of the arrogant wisdom of an older sibling who thought they'd seen the world.

"I'm not getting married," Tabitha announced. "Marriage is just a way for the patriarchy to oppress women into what they consider fitting roles."

"Don't let mama hear you say that," Eli warned.

"Why not! My opinion matters just as much as anyone else's," Tabitha demanded.

"You'd probably enjoy eating more with Kate than me, then," Eli smirked.

"Maybe I would," Tabitha giggled. "But I miss my big brother."

"And I miss my baby sister," Eli kissed her forehead again. "Tell me, how is your first semester of University going?"

Essie watched her husband disappear with his sister and tried to ignore Joanna's triumphantly smug look. It was Christmas after all. Essie busied herself with serving everyone and cleaning up after the crowd.

She found that she really was okay with watching everyone from the sidelines. Every now and then, the cousins and siblings she was sitting with would try to pull her into the conversation, but she would grace them with a few words and disappear back into the wallpaper. It was honestly exhausting to have to hobnob with them. She was okay to sit back and watch.

Especially so as the evening drew on and she started to feel ill. Really ill. Not the fake sickness that she would sometimes make up to avoid having Eli talk to her or attend social events. She was sweating, and her belly felt too heavy on her lower back.

It drew near to midnight, and Essie knew that she had several more hours to make it through before everyone would leave and she could retire. Mama Amy called the twins to her, and they set up a keyboard piano they had brought. Attarah sat down and played a short but beautiful piece and then started another one. Adiel joined her in singing and soon after Myra came over and joined the chorus. Some of the older children sang as well while some of the younger ones found their parents and favorite Aunts and Uncles, curling up on laps and in arms, drifting off to the strains of Silent Night.

Eli came up the stairs, holding the hand of Tabitha and they joined the song, her leaning on him and looking several inches up. Their eyes were locked as they sang. Their voices were joined to a greater piece but they were in their own little bubble world.

Essie crept away. She felt like an outsider. Eli was there with his brothers, beloved sisters, mother, father, and cousins that he grew up with as best friends. Even Kate and Andy were Eli's before they were hers. Her mother and Clay had had to leave already, and so her house was full of strangers. People who all claimed they loved her but they didn't know her. And she hardly knew them.

She sank into a soft gray armchair in the calm quiet of the guest bedroom. The bed was covered in everyone else's coats and wraps, and she couldn't make herself go and lie down in her and Eli's marriage bed while he and his family were out there happy and full of love. She loved Eli; she knew she did; she knew that she had to. It wasn't as if she could leave him or anything. She wrapped her arms around her stomach, feeling the baby through the worsted fabric of her dress. It felt way too tight, suffocatingly so. She wanted to take it off and fold herself into a flannel onesie. But she knew that it wasn't even an option. She lay back with a sigh and closed her eyes briefly. Just a few moments. Then she would go back out. Before she knew it, she was asleep.

Tabitha leaned against her favorite brother, and Eli tightened his arm around her shoulders. He looked down at her, eyes slightly closed and humming along to Attarah and Myra's duet. Eli's heart was full of joy, happily back with his family and so proud to have them all in his house.

"Eli! I asked if you have any preferences," Attarah called.

Eli's eyes snapped open. He hadn't even realized that he was falling asleep. His brothers laughed and clapped him on the shoulder. An almost asleep Tabitha was slumped against him, and he noted sadly the green looks that Attarah and Myra exchanged. Gently, Eli handed her off to Lucas who looked at him as if asking if he were serious. Tabitha, not nearly as asleep as Eli had thought, woke up as Lucas took her. The tall blond wife on Lucas's other arm made a face at him and Lucas handed Tabitha off to Samuel. Tabitha shook herself free of the youngest older brother and stood on her own, watching with arms crossed as Eli went over to see the other sisters. She scowled as her sister rivals for the best brother's affections stole him back with a laugh, a kind word, and their stupid bright blue eyes. Tabitha had always been able to charm her way to what she wanted with a well-placed wink and a hint of a smile. Men loved her.

Her father and oldest brother doted on her. It made her sisters dislike her and her brothers fear her.

Elias leaned on the piano and looked thoughtful. "Let me think. Play something cheerful! Look, everyone is falling asleep!"

Attarah smiled fondly at him and tucked her red hair behind one ear. Turning her fingers back to the keys and tuning Myra's voice, she started to play an upbeat carol that brought the room back to life.

"Beautiful!" Eli clapped at the end.

Attarah continued to play, but Myra broke away from the piano and caught Eli's hands. "Dance with me!" she laughed.

Eli twirled her, and she went off, pulling Lucas and Samuel into the dance. Lucas grabbed the hand of his wife and went around the piano with the others, skipping in a circle and singing in rounds. Eli retired to the couch to watch. He noticed Tabitha watched him possessively and was glad that she was caught in the circle. He loved her dearly, but he was glad to have a moment of quiet to just enjoy seeing everyone happy. He closed his eyes for just a brief moment, and when he opened them, Kate was leaning on his arm.

He grudgingly draped it around her as it started to go numb and afforded her a smile. "Hello, Katelyn. Glad you could make it."

"As am I. Where's your lovely bride? I was hoping to thank her in person, but she went off on her own before I could."

Eli suddenly looked around. Where *was* Esmeralda? "Uhhh," he said eloquently.

Kate raised an eyebrow. "Oh, I see."

"What?" Eli defended.

"You want to know what I think?" Kate began. Ignoring Eli's sardonic mutter of 'not really' under his breath. "She probably feels sick from being pregnant and sick of being ignored. I think that she got sick of watching you cuddle with your sisters. I sure did," she got up with a kiss on his cheek, smirking, "sisters before misters."

Essie started to wake up only moments before the door burst open. She could hear the voices approaching down the hallway.

"It's not fair!" a woman said with a sharp stubborn edge to her voice.

"Come here."

Essie heard the rustle of cloth, and then the door clicked open. She sat up just in time to see Andy with his arms loosely around one of Eli's twin sisters. Adiel maybe? Andy and her met eyes at the same time, and Essie waved weakly.

The twin quickly detached herself from Andy with a blush. Essie wouldn't have been suspicious otherwise, but that was strange. Andy took in the situation, pausing in his thoughtful way to look at the scene from both perspectives. Then he drew the girl to him and kissed her forehead. "Why don't you go back to see everyone, Addy?"

"But Andrew…"

"I'll be out in a moment," he promised. "I want to talk to my other cousin."

"In-law," Adiel looked at her distastefully. She, along with her other sisters (with the exception of overly mothering Jo), wasn't a fan of the blond girl who had swept her beloved brother away from the family.

"My cousin and friend," Andy said pointedly. "And your sister, Adiel."

She nodded, admonished, and gave a perfect little curtsy, leaving the room.

"You know Adiel and Attarah, right?" Andy chattered in the wake of the closing door. "They uh, they're the twins. Eli's little sisters. Of course, you've met them."

"They don't seem to like me," Essie noted.

"They'll come around," Andy soothed. "It's early days yet."

"Right…" Essie started to get up, but Andy quickly waved for her to go back to the chair. Essie chewed on her bottom lip. "Are you and her…" She glanced meaningfully at Andy and then at the door.

"Are we… oh! No! No, no, no! Don't worry! Just close!" Andy blushed.

"M'kay," Essie winked.

"No! Oh, gosh! Essie! She's like a sister to me. Like you are!"

"I didn't say anything differently," Essie held back a giggle.

"Okay Ess," Andy rolled his eyes. "Why are you in here alone? Hiding from your sisters-in-law?"

"Only partially," Essie admitted.

"What's the other part?" Andy folded his leg under the other and perched on the bed.

"Pregnant and tired," Essie forced a smile. "Don't worry."

"No issues with Eli? Everything is perfect in that little fairy tale, right?"

"Right," Essie said lightly.

"Are you going to come back out?" Andy asked. "It's nearly midnight. Come celebrate Christmas with us."

"Do I have to?"

"It's your party," Andy pointed out.

Essie groaned and heaved her tiny bulk out of the chair.

"Cheer up and enjoy this part! My mom says it'll only get worse!" Andy grinned.

"You're just making my day," Essie answered dryly.

Presently, Andy came out of the room, supporting Essie on one arm. He led her back out to the living room. Adiel met them in the hall and, sour-looking, made a polite nod to her hostess while taking Andy's other arm, making it look like the three had just been on a relaxing walk.

Essie noted with disgust that Eli was once again at the beck and call of Tabitha. Like Moses, she passed through a sea of torment, ignoring Tabitha's triumph and Joanna's pity and coming out on the other end calm and composed.

A few more carols were sung, and then the clocks all over the house began to ring. Children squealed and went running, looking for the watches and small clocks that had been hidden all over like a scavenger hunt. They ran back holding them and claiming prizes. The adults cheered and toasted and kissed each other merry Christmas.

Essie looked for Eli at the moment the clocks rang out. He was with Tabitha and as she watched pressed a kiss to the tip of her nose playfully. In the hubbub of noise, she couldn't hear, but they leaned close together and spoke quietly. Essie could only imagine what was being said. Hiding tears, she allowed Samuel to draw her into a hug and kiss her cheek. She was numb all over. Eli hadn't been there for her at all that night. Not when she was ill, not when she was feeling lonely and lost, and worst of all, he had put before her the trollop of a sister that Joanna said was taking her place. Essie had never hated him so much, and her heart had never ached as much as it did at that moment.

Kisses and hugs were all shared, and the families left one right after another as if afraid their cars would turn into pumpkins. Essie looked around the house and saw the dirty dishes everywhere. Scattered amidst them were cookie crumbs, napkins, forgotten mittens, and other odds and ends. Essie looked around the room, and the tears threatened to fall. She knew that she was just overtired, and she would feel better in the morning. Like an adult, she made the grown-up decision to sleep now and clean later. It wasn't as if she had anything better to do tomorrow.

Standing in their bedroom, she avoided the mirror as she struggled to unzip the stupid dress. She couldn't reach, and Eli was nowhere to be found. She called his name, desperately just wanting to pull off the thing and be able to sleep.

He came into the room at his own relaxed pace, yawning and smiling. "Hey, Esmeralda. Thanks for the great party. It was really nice to see my family."

"You're welcome," Essie ground out between clenched teeth. "Could you help me, please?" she begged, reaching for the zipper behind her.

Suddenly, Eli burst out laughing. Essie turned to him in annoyance, "Elias!"

"Sorry," he snorted. "It's just, Tabitha said that you looked like a red squash in that dress. She's kind of right."

Essie started to turn red with fury. "How... why... what... who... why would you say that!" she cried.

Eli looked at her. "It was just a joke, Essie. Don't take it so hard."

"You know, the dress I had before wouldn't have made me look like a *squash*!" she exclaimed, lip trembling. "But you're too damn lazy to get a job and get me a dress! So yes, I'm stuck with one that doesn't fit. Oh, and also I'm pregnant, Eli. That doesn't exactly help my figure!"

"Essie, stop it. You're acting like a child," Eli rolled his eyes, not making a move to help her.

Essie leaned forward, and the dress split down the back with an ear-cutting scream. She stepped out of it and threw it at the floor, hot drops of anger flowing down her cheeks. "Don't you dare tell me to calm down! I've had a shitty day. Did you even notice? I saw that you were rather preoccupied all evening. But it sucked, Elias Darcy, and you're making it worse. Just like you make everything worse!" she climbed into bed, sobbing too hard to put on pajamas.

Eli felt his heart sink a little bit, "Gem, maybe I shouldn't have teased you… but it was just a joke!" Her sobs only got louder. Eli climbed into bed with her and reached for her. Maybe all she needed to know was that he still loved her. Which he did. Even though it was hard sometimes.

The moment his hands touched her body, she pulled away, seething, "Get off of me!"

"Essie, I think that a little bit of cuddling will make us both feel better."

"You didn't even ask if I wanted it! It's not going to help *us*!" Essie cried.

"Okay, well it'll help me!" Eli reached for her again impatiently. "Ever think that I actually need physical comfort? That's how I see love! Can't you accept that! I need that tonight."

Essie sat up in bed, naked and beautiful even—or perhaps caused by—her six-month baby belly. Her green eyes were lit with absolute acrimony and the flames of promised hell. "Then go call Tabitha," she spat.

He gaped at her, the rage of her words setting in. Then, before either one could say anything, he swept out of the room toward the couch once more. Essie had no more tears that night. It was easier to be angry than sad.

Chapter 7

Even before Essie opened her eyes in the morning, the events of the night were still fresh in her mind. It was not going to be a very merry Christmas. Eli didn't even pretend to be interested in her that morning. They both got up and went to the kitchen at separate times, eating alone and tiptoeing around each other in the house. Or, not *actually* tiptoeing; Closer in fact to say being as loud as possible to irritate one another.

Around lunch time, Eli came upstairs and asked her what lunch was. Essie bit her lip, trying to decide what an appropriate reply was. She considered making another snap about Tabitha but reconsidered. That was too much. She chose, instead, to say nothing.

Eli spent the day working in the basement. He was careful to only use the power tools when he knew she was trying to do something that required a quiet house, such as watching TV or talking on the phone. He was so angry with her that he couldn't even speak to her. He wanted her to have a miserable day because he was.

When it came time for dinner, he asked what it was the same as he always would. Essie glared at him and ignored the question, turning away. Eli ordered take-out and ate downstairs by himself.

The day drew to a close and Eli, fed up with her silence, called Tabitha simply to spite his wife. She *was* spat, and halfway through the call unplugged the internet. When he asked what had happened, she shrugged and said that she was trying a new thing she had heard about where you turn off the internet before bed to help you sleep better.

Getting ready for the night, Elias pulled on his pajamas and moved toward the bed. Essie shot him a scathing look and said sharply, "I think you should move to the couch."

Hurt and angry, Eli retorted, "This is my bed! Thank you very much, Mrs. Darcy, but I seem to remember having bought it with my paycheck. In fact, I bought almost everything in this house. You've been in school, not working. When you married me, you came without fortune and only passed your financial burden from your mother's shoulders to me. I've been supporting you the whole time and you ought to be grateful for even having what you do."

"So I'll go to the couch then!" Essie snapped. "But I won't share a bed with you."

"You won't have to soon," Eli cried out, injured in mind and pride. "I'm leaving tomorrow. Greg and I need to go down south to get things set up for our business. It'll be a few weeks."

"Good! Go!" Essie yelled.

Eli grabbed a pillow and stalked out of the room. Essie helpfully threw the second one as hard as she could at the retreating back of his head as he slammed the door.

And thus passed their first Christmas together.

Eli woke up the next day sore from having slept on the couch for the past two nights. The brutal fight from the night before was still fresh in his mind, and the packed suitcase at the top of the living room stairs did little to help him forget the things that had been said. On his phone was a waiting text message from Greg. 'You still able to come?' Eli texted back 'Yes,' and started to get dressed.

He thought about going up the hall and saying good morning, but he couldn't bring himself to do it. He was still so angry. Maybe it would be a good thing for them to be separated for a bit while they cooled off. He picked up his bags and went down the stairs before the sun had reached its zenith. On a whim, he scrawled the address of the place where he and Greg would be staying. Underneath, in a wave of romanticism, he added, *I won't come back unless you tell me to. Love, Mr. Darcy.*

Essie got up and found the house still a mess from the party. Eli hadn't washed dishes or picked up anything from the living room a mess. In fact, instead of cleaning up, he had taken everything off of the couch and thrown it onto the floor to lie down. Essie bent to pick up a stack of plates when something caught her attention. There was nothing of Eli's on the floor. None of his clothing or personal belongings. The more she looked around, the more uneasy the room made her.

The knock on the door was sharp and urgent. Essie looked toward the door. She wasn't expecting anyone. The knock came again and then the door opened on its own. Kate stormed up the stairs and pulled Essie into the most vicious of hugs she had ever experienced. Essie stood shocked and still. "Kate?"

"I came to help you clean up, but this was on the door!" she brandished a sheet of notepaper.

Essie looked at her strangely. "What is it?"

Kate bit her lip. "You mean you haven't seen it?" She asked softly.

Essie shook her head. "What is it?" She said with a note of more concern.

Kate took her arm and guided her to the couch. She pushed her gently to sit down and only then did she hand her the note. Essie read over the two short lines on the paper. Kate watched her anxiously, a hand on her shoulder. "Essie? You okay?"

"I'm better than okay," Essie answered shortly. "So he's gone. That's fine," she choked on the last word and swallowed back any tears.

"Oh, honey," Kate rubbed her back. "You don't really want him gone."

"I do. Honestly, I do," Essie whispered. "That's why I'm crying. I want him gone. I want him gone forever and I want to go home. We fought, Kate. You wouldn't believe it if I told you, but we fought mercilessly. It was a bloodbath, and it was both of our faults, and there is no chance that he'll want me back. And I don't really want him!"

"Marriage is forever…"

"Don't preach at me, Katelyn!" Essie snapped.

Kate looked taken aback. She had seen angry Essie before but never directly at her. The two had never fought. They had quarreled but as far as Katie knew, the only person that Essie ever raised her voice at was Clayton. And now her friend was saying that she had yelled at Eli? Her precious Prince Darcy? Not to mention that Essie had spoken sharply to Kate herself. This wasn't like her at all and Kate didn't like it.

She looked around the room that had been part of the house the courting couple had so lovingly bought together, probably imagining where their babies would play and learn to take their first steps. Where they would snuggle together and watch movies on a cold night. Where they would live until they grew old and love and cherish one another. Certainly, they had never considered that their marriage would be destroyed before the first year was up.

Kate looked around the room, and she knew she was seeing the same things as Essie was. The beautiful ivy sculpted white trim around the edges of the pale-green walls was dirty with messy fingerprints and neglect. The Christmas tree still stood in its corner, drooping branches reaching for the floor and in many cases simply dropping off in pieces to the floor. Many presents lay under it still. They were things that Eli and Essie had been able to afford and were still unopened in the wake of their battle. The larger furniture lay askance, and the smaller chairs and footstools were scattered askew as if the room had seen a war. The blood was the blankets on the couch and personal items missing, proving that people had been injured. And grave injuries they were too.

Eyes finally settling on her friend's face, Kate reached out tentatively and brushed a tear-off of Essie's cheek. Essie hadn't had a chance to shower and get dressed before Kate had shown up. She was still in her pajamas, worn things that wouldn't do much against the cold. Essie was ashamed for Kate to see how poor they were. Kate didn't mention it, but she noticed. Hell, the entire family had noticed. The silence was the mutually agreed move. Essie's hair was down and lying matted around her shoulders. Her face, devoid of makeup or even traces of it seemed so young. Too young to be attached to the frail body boasting the rounded edges of the gross abdomen. Too young to be married.

"I don't even know him," Essie said, leaning against the back of the couch, massaging her lower back, and closing her eyes against spilling tears. The bright yellow of her hair against the gray face and green walls. "You were right. Right from the beginning. You said that I was too young and that we should wait. I was afraid that if I waited he would find someone else. I thought I was ready to be a wife and a mother. That's what they teach us, right?" Essie looked to Kate with pleading, confused eyes. "They always said as we were growing up that women were to be wives and mothers. To know our place and love it. Remember at our graduation, how many church friends told us that we were such modern women to be going to university? I was supposed to be ready to be a wife and mother."

Kate caught Essie's flailing hands, bewildered. "Yes, that's what they told us, but..."

"So why didn't it work out?" Essie sobbed.

Kate didn't know what to say. She wished that her mom or Mama Kyra were there to help. She wished that Joanna was there or Auntie Amy. She wished that she could go back and fix everything for the two people that she loved.

"Is this why you're never going to get married?" Essie hiccupped.

Kate nodded.

"I shouldn't have," Essie stared at her hands clasped over her bump. "I want out," she murmured.

"Ess..." Kate began. She knew that if any of the moms caught wind of this conversation there would be hell to pay, but she had to do something to help Essie. And Esmeralda needed more than a listening ear. "Essie, have you considered counseling?"

"For Eli?"

"For yourself? For both of you? Together or separate. It's healthy. Maybe it would help."

Essie shook her head. "He would never go."

"Maybe you should anyway?" Kate suggested tentatively.

Essie's brows came together. "Are you saying this is my fault?"

"Honey, these things take two."

Essie didn't answer. Then, "I couldn't. I'm stuck, Kate, and that's the short and long of it. He can stay in Florida forever for all I care, but at the end of the day, I am still his wife and he is still my husband, and we must cleave to each other. And oh, yes, we have a baby. I'm stuck, Kate!" Essie cried.

Kate shook her head, "You're not stuck. There's always a way out."

Essie swallowed. She could hardly bear to think about the word. She stammered and stared but Kate wouldn't say it for her. Katie would never be accused of putting the idea into her head. "Divorce."

Kate nodded.

Essie turned the idea over in her head. She grew up being taught that in hell, there was a special place for people who believed in abortion, homosexuality, and eating pork. There was a place there too for people who got divorced.

But she had met women who killed their babies that truly regretted it and lived the rest of their lives trying to atone. She had met gays who were kinder than most of the people at church and people who ate unclean meats and who loved God more than anyone else she had ever met. Was it possible that they wouldn't all burn for thousands of years?

"God... God hates divorce," Essie answered uncertainly.

Kate thought about her words carefully. "Yes, we should work hard to save our marriages. *But* having a good marriage isn't our number one goal. Our number one goal is to glorify God, and if staying in an abusive or unhealthy marriage is enabling sin and selfishness, that's a problem. I think your marriage is unhealthy honey. You two are fighting all the time and it's not nice."

"We have to stay together for the baby," Essie murmured.

"If that's the only reason you're still together, that's not right. The baby would grow up wanting to know why mama and daddy aren't talking to each other. You don't want that."

"What should I do?" Essie begged with a childlike need for guidance.

"First, we're going to clean up the house and get you showered and dressed. Then we're going to go look at some people online," Kate clapped her hands, making plans decisively.

"For Counselors?" Essie asked weakly.

"Yes... and divorce attorneys."

Eli couldn't focus on anything. He went through the motions, checked into the hotel room, went for dinner with

Greg, and went to meetings. He was careful and polite. He asked the right questions at the right times and answered with all the right words, but all the time, he couldn't stop thinking about Essie.

When he finally was able to get back to his room and lie down, he had been expecting to fall asleep so easily; he was drop-dead tired. But instead, he lay on his bed, staring at the ceiling and thinking about Essie. He was still so angry with her. She had said some unforgivable things to him. He had responded in turn, nicer even, dare he say than most people would have! But he had meant what he had said in his note. While it broke his heart to do so, he would stay away if that's what she wanted. He wouldn't divorce her—couldn't, had no reason to—but he wouldn't go back. Only if she specifically asked for him.

His phone rang suddenly, and Eli reached for it. The cheerfully profile picture of his little sister lit up the screen. Maybe that part was his fault. He shouldn't have made fun of her and spent the whole night with Tabitha. But still, she was his sister! And he loved her. Essie could have understood that he was just joking and let it be. He declined the call. Tabitha. Tabby was the one at fault here. She shouldn't have been so cruel to Essie.

Eli thought about calling Esmeralda. He wondered if she would even answer. He wondered if she was alone tonight with all of her emotions and fears and thoughts as he was. He wondered if she was thinking about him. He thought about her creamy white skin, all that flowing buttercup hair. The green eyes. Perfectly bright green. Like gems. And then he wondered if he even loved her anymore. His core answered quickly, but Eli was a man that was ruled by the head, not heart and he couldn't find an answer in his mind.

Kate wouldn't leave Essie alone that night. She grabbed her friend as soon as they were done scheduling a meeting with a lawyer for the next day and danced her across the room. Kate insisted that they celebrate. She called Alec and Andy and ever the social butterfly dressed Essie in the cutest dress she had that still fit and dragged her out of the house, saying that they were going to see some friends. They were no friends that Essie had ever heard of or met. Two of the bigger men looked at her appraisingly, and one made a snarky comment and looked as if he would make more before Andy came over and put an arm around her, shielding her from their gazes.

Before she knew it, they were going to a pub. "To dance, not to drink," Kate soothed her. Essie was not soothed. Andy got her a seat, making sure she was out of the way of the pressing crowd and protected her and the baby from harm. Quickly after that, they moved to another bar and another, and by the time, Andy was walking Essie up to the door, she had only four hours before she was scheduled to meet with her new lawyer friend to talk about divorces. It was a two-hour drive. There was no time for sleeping.

Essie showered and dressed and sat on the couch, watching TV like a zombie with a bowl of soggy breakfast cereal. None of them had drunk anything the night before but Essie was so bone-tired that she couldn't think. She started to nod off and her bowl of cereal tipped cold into her lap. She jumped up, sighing as she repeated the steps of showering, dressing, and eating, this time in a hurry, without TV, as she rushed to get into the car.

Eli's breakfast was served by a blonde with the darkest black eyes Eli had ever seen. They were shining black pools of darkness, reflected light and something mysterious in between. She had a sonsie, curvaceous figure that made him look twice. She touched his shoulder when she handed him a menu and winked as she passed to go to another table. She had served his yesterday morning too, and she was friendly. Very friendly.

On a break in the flow of traffic, she came over to him. "Hi, mind if I sit with you awhile?"

Eli, never comfortable with women, didn't know how to turn her away. Besides, he was a little bit lonely. He wouldn't mind some conversation. He not only nodded but also got up and pulled the chair out for her. She was surprised, looking boldly at him with those black eyes, lined today with a light sparkly aquamarine pencil.

"A gentleman," she winked coyly.

Eli was silent, not knowing if it would be appropriate to thank her? Or laugh maybe. He settled on extending his hand. "My name is Elias."

"Lena," she smiled, shaking his hand.

"A pleasure to meet you."

"The pleasure is all mine," she answered looking him over. "What brings you here?"

"Business."

She twisted a strand of her golden hair. Not as golden as Essie. And Esmeralda's curls were much more interesting. But she was pretty. Eli could admit. "What kind of business?" she pushed.

"I own a legal firm," Eli disclosed.

Her shimmering eyes widened. "Well, that's fancy. My sister is a lawyer."

"It's an interesting job," Eli answered politely.

Another couple came into the restaurant and Lena stood obviously reluctant. "I'll be right back," she said, smiling.

As she got the couple settled, Eli stood and stacked his plates. When Lena came back, she had changed out of uniform and perched, leaning on Eli's table. "One of the other girls will clear your dishes—it looks like you're done?—I'm just now off of shift. Can I walk you up to your room?"

Eli shrugged and nodded. "Sure?"

Lena took his arm gracefully, looking at him with a sort of predatory appreciation. "Thanks."

Essie got into the car and turned the key in the ignition. The vehicle started over, and she slowly drove down the driveway. Drunk tired, she moved onto the road. The first trouble arose when she slowed to a stop at the sign by the corner of the intersection. Paused before the stop sign, she closed her eyes for a moment, which turned into two, and then she was asleep. A car behind her drove up and honked loudly. Essie jumped in her seat and maneuvered back onto the road. The vehicle leaned on their horn, shooting around and past Essie.

She shook her head, frightened awake. She couldn't fall asleep. In the back of her head, she had a firm idea that she probably shouldn't be driving at all. It wasn't sane. But she laughed to herself, giddy on sleeplessness and thinking that she was or at least soon would be free to do whatever she wanted. Stay up late, dance, see her friends and sleep in late. She just had to make it to the destination of this car ride.

Essie turned on the radio to help her stay awake. The car was tuned to a station of Christian pop. She had a sudden flashback to weeks ago when, at church, she and Eli had been gifted with a beautiful golden-edged, white-leather covered Bible with their names embossed into the top from a fond church member who was apologetic that she had been unable to make it to their wedding. She reminded them to keep God in the center of their marriage and, in the way of pious old ladies, blessed them liberally and kissed Essie's stomach without asking. Essie's stomach churned and she quickly turned off the radio. The car fell silent.

Maybe the silence was the reason she started to drift off again. Maybe it was the way she was actively avoiding thinking about him. Maybe it was really just how completely exhausted she was. Whatever it was, Essie started to drift off again. Fortunately, she was not on an embankment road or close to any drop-off. She was on a simple highway. The car sliding sideways was what woke her up. It rolled once and she screamed. She gathered her wits as best she could and tried to pull the car out of the way of oncoming traffic. The vehicle kept on rolling.

Eli thought that Lena might be standing a little too close to him. He inched away, and she followed. He thought to himself that he was maybe a little shy around women, but he wasn't stupid. He was afraid that he had maybe gotten himself into quite a predicament. He tried gesturing more with his left hand. He pushed the button for the elevator with it and waved it while speaking but if Lena noticed his wedding band, she didn't react or change her behavior. Eli was astounded. How was it possible that she hadn't seen it? And it couldn't be that she was just ignoring it! What woman in her right mind would try for another woman's husband?

Eli stepped away from her to open the door to his room. He was slow as she kept up her endless chatter. He hoped that she would stay inside but Lena—as he subconsciously had presumed she would—followed him inside the room. She settled onto the couch and asked for a glass of water, which Eli brought her.

He lingered in the doorway, wondering how long she would stay. He looked back at her, and she had her head bent toward the ground. He had a sudden glimpse of another blonde who looked down coyly just like that, only when in her best moods. Esmeralda. What on earth would she think of him? Lena tossed her hair, and Eli saw Tabitha. What would Tabby think of him? Lena got up and without meeting his gaze said, "Don't worry about the glass; I'll take care of the dishes," Joanna and his mama sprang to mind. Lena, who brought characteristics of all the women he loved into the room, had to go because he couldn't bear to think of how they would react. A part of his mind demanded what on earth he thought he was doing wrong. The bigger part answered sharply that he had no right to have a woman in his bedroom other than his wife.

Lena appeared at his elbow and touched it gently. He jumped and turned to face her, and when he did, she touched him carefully, running a hand through the dark hair framing his face.

He was caught in a moment of terror and sculpture-like couldn't move. "Lena… I am married," he said, standing stock still.

She ran her hands over his chest. "You didn't mention your wife earlier…" She said mildly. Not accusing or angry. Still in that soft voice as though it were all wrapped in silk.

Eli wanted to take a step back. Away from her. She was so much like Esmeralda but so different. Better in some ways? He wished that Essie had taken more of an interest in physical touch. He wished Essie had taken charge like this. Eli considered himself a dominant person, but there was something so attractive about the way she was so confident. "I… I…"

"You…" she murmured leaning in and touching his nose with hers.

"I meant to mention her…" Eli answered pitifully. He hated the way his voice sounded.

"Is that why you're really here? I've seen your kind before," Lena said kindly. She led him by the hand to the couch and settled herself into his lap, wrapping his arms around her slender waist. "Men who come to hotels like this one with a made-up excuse about why they are away from wives they don't talk about. Baby, I know why you're here."

"I'm not here to cheat on my wife… she's… I love her."

"So why aren't you home?"

"She doesn't want me there," he said softly, looking down at the ground.

"So she wouldn't even care if we spent some quality time together," Lena wheedled, pressing a hand to his chest.

Eli didn't move, letting her hands roam over his shoulders and play with the top buttons of his dress shirt.

But when she murmured "Elias" with a voice of passion, he pushed her away.

"Lena, I'm faithful to my wife," he gently moved her away from him and stood up, comfortable in the several inches he rose over her. Those same inches reminded him of the petite little wife he had left behind. He was big enough to protect her. He should have protected her. She was far away in their house, all alone and likely frightened. He was her husband, it was his job to make sure she was never scared and he was failing miserably. He should go home… But then, he thought if she didn't want him there, he would be doing more harm than good.

He ushered Lena out of the rooms as gently as he could, and when she was gone, he sat on the couch and buried his face in his hands, thinking about their wedding day. This was not at all where he had seen this going that day. He had no idea that, in less than a year, his marriage would turn into such a mess. He thought about the good times that they had shared. If he had known it would come to this, would he still have married her? When all was said and done, he wanted to say yes. He still loved her. He still would have wanted the time that he spent with her.

Eli leaned on the table with his head in his arms. He wondered if it could all be fixed. He demanded of himself whether or not he would fight for her. He challenged if he would possibly go home and take her back. They had both said things in the heat of anger that could hardly be retracted. Knowing how bitterly they could argue, he wondered if they could possibly make it any longer. Maybe it was better that they figured out that they were not compatible and separated now while they were young.

Eli had never believed in soul mates. He had always agreed that marriages took work and had to be held together carefully. If they separated now there would be another wife for him, he knew that. And another husband for Essie. The idea made him sick, and he started to cry in the wake of the thought that he would see her marry another man. He cried because he knew he still loved her so much and couldn't bear the thought of losing her. He cried for his childish hopes and dreams for their marriage. He cried for the unborn baby who would grow up without their daddy. He cried for their unborn future possibilities.

Essie closed her eyes in terror. Her mom had always told her that if she were in an accident and she lost control of the vehicle, pulling frantically on the wheel to try and turn it would only make it worse. She let go of the steering wheel and in the last few seconds of the spinning car that she remembered, everything slowed, and she started to remember.

Her fifth birthday party was the first one that she remembered. It was only a few days before she was scheduled to start school. Her daddy had stood with her mom in the back of the room, arms around each other as she sat opening her gifts. Her aunt was playing the piano, and other family and friends were gathered around laughing and smiling. The room was warm with love and laughter.

After her first week of school, she came home one day crying about something that had happened. Her daddy picked her up, and she cuddled with him on the couch where he was lying down. He held her while she cried and kissed her. He sang to her and made her laugh. She asked him why he was on the couch, and he explained that he was feeling sick. Essie remembered that he had been spending a lot of time lately lying on the couch. Her mom bustled in before she could ask any more questions. Kyra brushed her into her own room and told her to let her father rest. That night Essie woke up to the sound of crying. She crept into the living room and found her mom crying over her dad's still body. When Kyra saw Essie lingering she pulled the tiny blond to her and explained tearfully that her daddy had loved her very, very much, but he had to go to sleep and he would wake up again when Jesus came back. Then they would be a happy family together. Essie cried with her mom, not understanding why her dad wouldn't wake up and because her mama was sad. They didn't let her go to the funeral.

Seven years later, Essie nervously approached her mom quietly and told her that she wanted to buy a bra. Kyra was thrilled that the girl felt she could talk to her about the matter and answered that she would clear her Monday schedule so they could go right after school. When Kyra picked her up that night, she had Matthew, her second husband, with her. Essie shrank back, embarrassed and demanding why he had come. Determined to win the little girl's affections, Matt tried to hold her hand as they walked into the store. A teen, she was angry at Matthew for coming and trying to replace her father, and at her mother for allowing him to. Essie tried on the first bra and walked out of the fitting room with it on to show her mom. Matthew nearly had a heart attack and after which he rarely said more than four words together to her or tried to father her until his death in a car crash two years later.

When she was fifteen, Essie had been invited out with some of the more popular kids at the school. Essie often got such invitations as Kate was part of the in-crowd. This time, the group was going bridge jumping. Kate and Essie were in their first year at the private school, and most of the kids were in their third or fourth year. The older group came up with the idea of a formal initiation for the two younger girls. After a few jumps each, the older students said that they could be official members of the group if they would jump off of the bridge. The two (who had been, up to this point, sunbathing contentedly) were shocked but willing. The sun was just starting to set. Essie remembered the brilliant orange and purple of the sky. They got ready to jump at the edge of the bridge in the short skirts and blouses of the school's uniform. One of the bolder seniors called out that if they jumped in all those layers of cloth the current would pull them under. The others quickly joined in the call that they should take them off. Accordingly, Essie and Kate stripped to their underwear and, holding hands, jumped.

The icy water swirled around them, cold and hard as shards of glass. When they came up for air, the older students were standing around the top of the bridge cheering at them shivering in their panties. They swam to the edge of the river, pulling themselves out and dreading the walk through the parking lot and back up to where the others were. Somehow, Andy had found out where they would be and was waiting for them in the parking lot. He wrapped Kate in his jacket and draped his wool sweater around Essie, bundling them silently into his warm truck. They both got hopelessly sick and he quietly brought soup over to Essie's house every day faithfully, not explaining one word to Kyra.

Her mom had had one good boyfriend. His name was Ethan, and he had made Essie laugh from the beginning, no matter how predisposed she was to dislike him. He was wonderful to her, bringing her a rose whenever he bought Kyra a bouquet. He accompanied her to her grade 10 semi-formal daddy-daughter dance. He dressed to match her and brought her an orchid corsage. That night he broke up with her mom and left the house, kissing her on the cheek and leaving her standing on the porch in her blue satin dress, heartbroken. Essie became determined not to love anyone else or to trust any other man her mom introduced to her. Her fears proved understandable. After Ethan, her mom got engaged to Clayton.

Essie remembered meeting Elias at her graduation party. On their first date, he had taken her out for a full romantic night. They watched the Sound of Music, and he had sung to her as he taught her to dance the Laendler. She remembered every date after that, the poetries and flowers and chocolates. She remembered the late-night conversations that continued for hours. He remembered the one spontaneous night he had shown up at her house after midnight and thrown pebbles at her window, asking her to come out and stargaze with him. They had lain on a quilt while he pointed out constellations, and then she fell asleep and he woke her up to ask her if he could carry her back to the truck. She thought about the day they had gone to church together and he had introduced her to Pastor James as "the future Mrs. Darcy."

Their wedding, her graduation, the discovery of her pregnancy all flew past in her mind. She remembered their first fight and making up for it. Then her eyes flew open, and she found that, the split second later, though it had felt like an hour, had thrown her into another roll in the vehicle. Just before the car smashed into a guardrail Essie thought about her mom and Elias and cried that it would end like this. Then on impact, she wrapped her arms around her belly and screamed before she couldn't scream anymore.

Chapter 8

Kyra was just waking up lazily with no plans for the day, though it was mid-afternoon. She was lying in bed with Clay's arm thrown restlessly over his face. She looked at him and smiled. She was glad that she had found love once again in this good God-fearing man. Before she got out of bed, she closed her eyes and prayed. She started with a prayer of thanksgiving that her Lord had breathed life into her once again that morning. She went on to ask blessings on Clay and Esmeralda and Elias and their precious little baby. She asked God to protect her girl and bring her back to visit her sometime. Kyra worried about Essie. It had been weeks since they spoke. Kyra feared that she was having a hard time adjusting to married life but didn't know how to help her. She seemed off at the Christmas party but Clayton had wanted to leave and they hadn't had a chance to exchange anything more than pleasantries.

The phone rang in the stillness, and Clayton grunted, reaching over and grabbing it. "Hello?" At the muffled response he sat up sharply. "You're from where… okay, hold on, here she is," he handed the phone to his wife.

"Kyra Landry. How may I help you?" Kyra watched, confused as Clay rushed to get dressed. The male voice on the other end explained more through the calm tone and what he didn't say than what he did.

"Good afternoon, Ma'am. My name is Fox Idris; I'm a paramedic emergency worker at Newcastle Hospital. I'm calling to ask if you are affiliated with Mrs. Esmeralda Darcy? Yours was the first number we came across in her pocketbook. Do you know who we should get in touch with? A family member?"

"I… I'm her mother…" Kyra gasped.

"Okay, thank you, Ma'am. Could you come to the hospital? We need you to sign some paperwork," the man said gently.

"Yes, I can be there in 20 minutes," Kyra answered in a small voice. She was already starting to get dressed before she hung up.

Clay held out a coat for her. "What's going on?"

"I don't know," Kyra answered, out of control of her thoughts and actions. "They didn't tell me anything! Only that Essie's in hospital and got there by ambulance! They want me to fill out paperwork. Clayton, she's dead," Kyra moaned. "She's dead, and they want me to identify her body! I can't! I can't do it!"

Clay gathered her tightly against him for a moment then released her quickly. "If she were dead they would have told you immediately. Come on. She's fine, and she's going to continue to be fine enough to drive me batty all through my old age."

A quiet hum broke over her in waves. Essie was surrounded by sterile blankets and bustling figures in white. Her abdomen hurt. As she came to consciousness, she began to register pain all over. She felt a sharp pain in parts of her body she didn't know existed. But the gut-wrenching pain in her belly felt like nothing she had ever experienced before. She couldn't remember anything after the car skidding into the guardrail of the highway. Where had she been headed…? Oh, right. Divorce lawyer. Suddenly her marriage didn't seem like the biggest issue anymore. She hurt so bad.

"Am I having my baby?" she croaked. No one seemed to hear her. She wondered for a moment if she had grown up with the wrong beliefs, and she was dead and in heaven after having died without waiting for God to come back. But no… in heaven, she wouldn't feel this kind of agony.

"Please…" she started to beg. Her voice came out in a whisper and trailed off.

There was suddenly a person at her bedside. "Hi, I am Nurse Sophia! How are you feeling?"

"Terrible," Essie whimpered. "Where am I?" She looked around and as her eyes adjusted to the light and she felt a rush of humiliation. What a dumb question. "It's a hospital, right?"

"That's right!" the nurse said cheerfully. "I'm glad to see that you are able to make out your surroundings. Do you know your name?"

"Essie… Esmeralda Landry Darcy."

"I'm pretty sure you're right!" Sophia nodded checking her chart. "So, Mrs. Darcy—do you mind if I just call you Essie?—Essie, you were in a pretty serious automobile accident. I can't tell you much until the doctor comes, but can I get you anything?"

Essie closed her eyes briefly against a throb of pain. "What's wrong with me?" she gasped.

"Like I said, I can't tell you much," Sophia's smile never faltered. "But the doctor will be here soon. We'll have you all patched up. Is there anything I can do for you right now? Do you want us to make any phone calls?"

"My…" Essie halted. Her husband or her mother or Kate or Joanna or Mama Amy. Who did she want? "My mother?" she said hesitantly.

"We already contacted a Mrs. Kyra Landry. Is that her?" Sophia asked kindly.

"Yeah," Essie whispered.

"Anyone else?" The nurse encouraged. "The files say that you are married, but we couldn't find his number. We only found Kyra's in your folders. Do you want us to contact him? And also, they suggested that you should put your medical records up to date."

Essie thought about Elias's note to her. He was far away and at work. If what they said was true, she would be out of there soon enough, and he would never need to know. Besides, he always hated it when she interrupted his work. She couldn't do that. "No, please don't," she answered.

The nurse looked surprised but didn't question to Essie's relief. "Okay… are you going to be okay alone for a bit? The doctor and your mom will be here soon," she walked away and left Essie in the peaceful torment of her thoughts.

She realized with a jolt that she still loved him. She loved him dearly. But it didn't make sense! She screamed in her head as she considered the possibility. She was on the way to see a divorce lawyer! Rationally, she tried to think it through. It was completely possible that she could still love him but shouldn't be married to him. Marriage had little to do with love. It was about working together, and she couldn't work with him. And clearly, he couldn't work with her. She drifted into a misery-filled coma in the throes of tears.

"Baby!" Kyra called softly, her voice full of fear. She reached down and brushed tears off the cheeks of her pale daughter. "Wake up, darling…"

Essie opened her eyes at her mother's voice, "I wasn't sleeping, Mama. Just resting." Kyra bent and kissed her gently but even as soft as the embrace was, Essie flinched away. "Sorry, Mama. It… I… everything hurts."

"Don't apologize!" Kyra exclaimed. "I just want you to be okay!" To her horror, Kyra began to cry. Essie had only seen her cry twice before; at the deaths of her husbands. Both of them were embarrassed and uncomfortable. "When I got the call," Kyra started to explain, "I thought you were… dead. They told me I had to come in and identify your body and fill out papers."

Essie looked past her to the doctor. "Your people frightened my mom," she said reproachfully.

He smiled soberly at her, "My sincerest apologies, Mrs. Darcy," he made a slight bow to Essie and her mother. "Ladies, could we talk now about your injuries?"

Kyra nodded, and Essie waited in silence.

"In the crash, you sustained a very serious injury. We call it 'Contrecoup' injury. It's also known as placental abruption. Placental abruption can cause the placenta to be prematurely detached from the uterine wall, which cuts off blood flow to the placenta. That's a delicate attachment, and it doesn't take a lot of force to detach the placenta. This is, obviously, a critical medical condition that can be fatal not only to the baby but also to the mother's health in serious and potentially life-threatening danger. Internal bleeding, severe abdominal pain, and dizziness can all result from a case of placental abruption."

Essie stared in horror. "Is my baby alive?"

"Right now you are in the ICU. It would seem as though you have not received any dangerous injuries, although, notice that your arm is wrapped up; the wrist was minorly fractured when caught, pinned, between the steering wheel and yourself. You cannot stay in the ICU. We are going to move you to the maternity ward as soon as possible. We think that for the time, being the best thing you can do would be to have the baby sooner. We are going to get access to your examinations…" The doctor ignores her and continues, looking down at his chart, "How far along are you?"

"Six and a half months!" Essie exclaimed in frustration. "Sir! Does that mean my baby is alive and well?"

"Hmm? Oh! Oh, yes. For the time being."

Essie held back her tears of relief. The doctor explained that they would schedule an induction within the week so that she could still experience a natural birth. He told her to call them now if there was anyone that she would want with her. Then he hesitated for a moment and said, "Mrs. Darcy, this condition, if not treated properly, can sometimes result in other long-term side effects."

"Like what?" Kyra asked anxiously.

"Right now it's not looking like there will be other babies," the doctor answered gently.

Essie didn't fully understand. "Sir?"

"You wouldn't be able to carry any other baby to term."

"Oh," she whispered.

"We're going to do our best to make sure that this one comes safely and that you are also alright. Okay? It's okay. We're going to take care of it all," the doctor touched her arm reassuringly. "We're going to move you this evening. I'll leave you two here to take this all in for a while. Ring for Sophia if you need anything."

He left the room while Kyra and Essie joined hands. Esmeralda weeping softly. "I was so scared for you, sweetheart," Kyra murmurs.

"I was so scared mama. I thought I was going to die," Essie cried.

Kyra took in her tear-stained face and arms protectively around her stomach. "Esmeralda, darling, are we going to talk about why they called me and not Elias? And why they haven't called him yet? He should be here by now. And if I know the dear boy, if he was in Japan and they had called him only an hour ago, he would have found a way to be here by now," she said in her shrewd way.

"I didn't want him here, Mama," Essie admitted. Kyra didn't say anything in response, waiting for Essie to continue. "Because… he didn't want to be here. He left early yesterday morning. We fought. Like you would never ever believe. He left on a business trip and left me a note saying he wouldn't come back unless I wanted him to. He didn't even say goodbye!" Essie's voice climbed as she reached a pitch of hysteria.

"Esmeralda, breath!" Kyra said sharply.

Essie answered as she always would have as a girl. With instant obedience, she took several quick, calming breaths. "Mama, I was talking to Kate and we booked an appointment for me to go see a divorce attorney. That's where I was headed when I was in the accident."

Kyra squeezed her fingers. "I think the Lord had a special plan for you, Esmeralda. And it didn't include divorce after less than a year."

"Mama, our relationship isn't going to work out. He left, Mama," Essie averted her eyes from her mother.

"Esmeralda, look at me. Marriages can't be ended as easily as breaking up with a boyfriend. You are Mrs. Landry-Darcy and he is Mr. Landry-Darcy. You are yoked together in God's sight. You can't just separate and leave it forever. God said that marriage was a sacred union to be broken only in the most severe of consequences."

"Mama, I don't need the lecture," Essie looked her in the eye. Kyra's eyes were as bright green as Essie's but with golden brown flecks around the iris. They were as hard as emerald stones and as beautiful. Clever with age and sharp with knowledge.

"I think you do. I see this story so often in your generation. You all give up too easily. You have divorce lawyers and the internet and high-speed Wi-Fi and no shame. You all think you can get away with anything and everything for nothing. Esmeralda, I didn't raise you that way. You can't just give up."

"I don't want to, Mama!" Essie raised her voice. "You think this is what I want! I didn't walk down the aisle thinking, 'ah yes, I would really love to end up hating my life with this man I love and getting a divorce before I'm 23. That would be great!' I didn't ask for any of this! But he doesn't want me anymore."

"He didn't say that, Ess," her mom responded softly.

"Yes, he did. He left," she cried.

"You said the note was that he wouldn't come back unless you called for him. He likely feels that you sent him away and don't want him back. He thinks he's doing what you want."

The two were quiet for a while before Kyra continued, "So I think that the choice is yours to make. If you want him back, Esmeralda, call him and let him know."

They fell into silence again as a nurse came to take Essie's blood pressure and temperature. Essie didn't know what to say. "I love him, Mama. I still do."

"Of course, you do," Kyra touched her cheek. "When was the last time you prayed with your husband?" She suddenly asked.

Essie looked thoughtful. She couldn't remember. They had prayed together at the beginning of meals… sometimes. When they weren't arguing. They used to get up and read the Bible in the mornings together when they would open and close with prayer but hadn't done that in a very long time.

"I see," Kyra answered with a ghost of a smile. "I think that should be a priority, love. Make God the center of your relationship. Without him, you can't make it anywhere. It's like a tree. Elias and you are the branches and your coming baby is the beautiful blossom. It all works out when the pieces are all talking to each other, but when they stop communicating, God, the trunk of the tree, is cut out, everything falls apart. You need each other. And you need God."

"Yes, Mama."

"So tell me, Esmeralda. Do you want your husband home with you?"

"Yes," Essie said firmly, without hesitation. "Yes! Yes, I do!"

"So call him. And tell him you love him."

Eli walked into his meeting. His suit was pristine and his presentation immaculately prepared. Outwardly, he was perfectly ready to present to the board of angels and get his and Greg's idea off the ground. It would all be fine.

Inwardly, he wanted to cry and scream, or rather, *continue* crying and screaming, he had already done a fair bit. He was hardly half an hour into the introductions of the seminar when the front desk secretary came up to him with a note. He had missed a phone call. Eli looked nervously at his watch he had about ten minutes before he was scheduled to present. He couldn't afford to mess this up. Literally.

"I told you to hold my calls," Eli murmured to the lady.

"I'm sorry, I thought that this one was important. It's from an Esmeralda Darcy from the Newcastle Hospital."

Eli's head snapped up. "What did she say? And from the hospital?" Greg squeezed his arm, warning him to be quiet, but Eli had to know what she had said.

"Here's the note," the woman handed him the slip of paper.

Scanning it quickly he jumped up, scraping his chair against the floor loudly. It echoed through the conference room and he apologized quickly as he hurried out, not even seeing Greg, bright red with embarrassment.

In the hall, he turned to the secretary again and demanded, "When is the next flight to Toronto."

She looked down dumbly at the ground and answered slowly… "I'll have to check, I'll be a mo—"

"Never mind," Elias pulled out his cell phone. "I'll check myself," he snapped. The report came back that he had 2 hours. He was on his phone in an instant, messaging Essie that he would be there soon. She had sent that she was in the hospital and wasn't injured, but she was going to be having their baby soon and wanted him there. She had said that she loved him and was praying for his safe return.

It had been a quiet day in the maternity ward. Nurse Sophia even had had time to take a coffee break before she left for the day. She leaned on the desk of her friend working as a secretary and they chatted for a while. The two were getting ready to go home after the shift when the man burst in. Sophia and her friend exchanged looks. He was the entire stereotype of the dark, dreamy billionaire. He was dressed in an impeccable suit, dark hair hazing over dark eyes. Sophia and her friend made looks at each other and Sophia jumped up, moving toward him. "Hi, I'm a nurse here, Sophia Winston. Can I help you?"

"I'm looking for someone…" he stammered.

"Who might that be?" she asked shyly.

"Esmeralda Darcy. I… I need to see her!"

Sophia thought about the pale, frightened young woman she had left earlier that day. Her heart dipped a little bit. Husband? By the way, he was looking around anxiously, definitely either husband or relative. "I can show you to her room," Sophia offered. "Mind if you give me a name to introduce you?"

"Elias Darcy. I'm her husband," he added with nyctophiliac urgency.

"Of course," Sophia sighed. Her friend made a face at her. All the good men were married.

Eli followed the nurse to a set of doors swinging back and forth as people bustled away. The nurse looked concerned. "Wait here for a moment. I'll go see if she can see you."

She disappeared into the chaos. Eli could only hear people talking and calling loudly over one another. He suddenly heard Mama Kyra over all of their voices. The gentle, frightened strains of his wife's voice drew to him from behind the doors. It took every ounce of self-control he had not burst into the room and pull her into his arms to protect her from everyone. He held himself back

A moment later, Kyra came out of the room with a sober expression and a hurried lilt to her step. "Mama Kyra!" Eli called. She turned her blond head to him and the look of relief was immediate and so much like Essie's that he couldn't breathe for a moment. He had to see her. He was so worried.

Mama Kyra came to him and hugged him fiercely, crying onto his shoulder, "Thank God!" over and over again.

Eli held her and cried over her head. "What happened! Is she okay?"

Kyra stepped back from him and stared into his brown irises. "They didn't tell you anything?"

Eli shook his head. "Please, is everything okay?"

"She was in a car accident. A severe one. She is going to be okay, I think. They are going to induce her so she can deliver the baby. They want him or her born right away. She has a condition from the crash... Contra... something..."

The doctor stepped into the hall with Nurse Sophia at his side and another woman in white on the other hand. "Contra Coup Injury. Placental abruption. The placenta separated from the uterine lining too early. Mrs. Landry, we'd like to talk to Mr. Darcy and catch him up to speed. And we're sure that he'll want to see his Lady."

Kyra kissed both of his cheeks and murmured to him, "Clayton is with her right now. He is doing his best to keep her happy and calm, but you can guess how well *that* is going. I am stepping home to get her a nightgown and robe, slippers, that sort of thing. I'll be back soon. Promise."

Eli was loath to let her go.

"Be brave now," Kyra scolded gently. She squeezed his hands. "We need to have a good chat one of these days, you and I. But until then, call your mama and sisters to come to be with her. There's no shame in needing your mama, Son," she said softly.

"Okay," he whispered as she slipped out of his arms and hurried off proudly and quickly. His hands were still outstretched to her as she left the hall and the doctor cleared his throat toward him.

"Sir? Good afternoon, I am Dr. Church. This is Obstetrician and Gynecologist Laura Bird."

Eli shook hands with both of them nervously. "Elias Darcy. Is my wife okay?"

The two doctors exchanged a look. It was the kind of look that a flight attendant might make when announcing everyone should put on their oxygen masks. It was the kind of look that you never want to see on your doctor. Eli suddenly felt his knees go weak.

"Ms. Esmeralda, after being diagnosed with Contra Coup, started to develop a very high blood pressure. She complained of a headache that wouldn't go away," the obstetrician said calmly as if she dealt with this kind of thing every day! Eli was terrified and she was acting like it was all just routine! "That's when they called me. Mr. Darcy… has your wife been to a single one of her checkups since she discovered the pregnancy?"

"No… her religious beliefs…" Eli said numbly.

"Ms. Esmeralda has another, significantly, more serious condition called pre-eclampsia. Risk factors for pre-eclampsia include obesity, prior hypertension, older age, and diabetes mellitus. It is also more frequent in a woman's first pregnancy and if she is carrying twins. The underlying mechanism involves abnormal formation of blood vessels in the placenta among other factors."

"What are you saying?"

"She was carrying twins. One of the babies died in uterus, about two months ago, it would seem."

"And the other baby?" Eli asked anxiously.

"The condition is very dangerous," Dr. Bird sketched abstractly.

"What does that mean? What do you mean?" Eli exclaimed.

"We are going to induce immediately and administer a blood pressure medication called labetalol to improve the mother's condition before delivery. The best thing now is for the baby to be born," the OB/GYN spoke carefully.

"But everything will be fine, right? It has to be. I haven't seen her in a few days, can I see her?"

Eli got the feeling of being brushed off and pushed unimportantly to the side as the two doctors and the nurse left him standing in the hallway alone. The still bubble gave him too much time to think about what was happening. He came back to apologize to his wife and make sure she was okay. It was all moving way too fast.

As if to make his point, the OB/GYN came back out of the swinging doors with a clipboard. "Mr. Darcy? Unfortunately, the drugs haven't done much to bring her blood pressure down. We have scheduled immediate emergency surgery."

Eli's head spun. "A surgery… a Cesarean section surgery?"

"Yes, Sir," she looked at him honestly, letting some light of worry shine through. "Mr. Darcy, I have to tell you that in cases like this our protocol is to save the mother first."

"Save the mother!" Eli cried. "What do you mean? What is happening?"

"Does your wife have a DNR…"

"A Do Not Resuscitate? Why would she need one?"

"It's a very dangerous situation and a delicate procedure. We're going to do our best to make sure everything goes smoothly. You can come in and see her in a few moments. I just need to collect her information from the desk," the doctor hovered over his arm. "I know it's scary. I can't promise anything except that we're going to do our very best to make sure everything is okay. Okay? Be brave for her now," she walked away without waiting for an answer.

Eli stood alone in the hall once more. Be brave. Be strong. He could do that. He had to. He had to be strong for her. Even as he thought he was determined to do so, he got a lump in his throat and couldn't hold back tears. A drop slid down his cheek, chased by another in an anti-pluviophile waterfall.

The whole time that he was standing there he was praying fervently. "Please God, don't take her from me. Forgive me for everything I've done. Please let her live. If you take her away from me and give her to someone else, I can live with that. But let her live. Lord, please," he pleaded quietly. He fell to his knees on the tiled floor, hands clasped and remembering her. He swore that if God granted her to come back to him, he would be more careful. He would never be rude to her again. He would never ever raise his voice at her. He would never even spank their kids. "Just, *please* God, bring her home to me."

He drew out his cell phone, weighing his options. He had to call someone. He had to tell someone what was happening and how he was feeling. He wanted his mother. He dialed her number with shaking fingers and put the phone to his ear. She answered on the second or third ring.

"Elias?"

"Mama?" Eli began, his voice cracking. "Essie is sick. Really sick and… I'm scared, Mama." More tears fell down his face.

"Do you want me to come to be with you?" she answered immediately.

Eli felt like a girl, sobbing as much as he was at such a simple answer. There was nothing demeaning in it. She never berated him for acting weak, she didn't criticize. She only offered to come to be with him. "Yes, please," Eli choked out.

It was as soon as he hung up the phone that Dr. Bird was back. "Mr. Darcy? Right, this way. Gown and gloves..." They were passed to him by nurses on hand and then he was led through the doors.

Essie was lying there on the gurney, pale as can be with a gray pallor to her face and artificial pink pinched into her cheeks. Her hair tumbled around her shoulders, still matted with sweat from the car accident. She had heavy bluish bags under her green eyes. She looked absolutely exhausted, filthy, and terrified. She was beautiful.

Essie lay on the hospital bed, her heart beating out of control. She would be able to calm herself down and then think back on the day's events, and it would spike again. She had heard one of the nurses mutter about a Mr. Darcy. Her heart skipped a beat. Was he here? He said he was coming; could he already be here? Was he angry that she hadn't contacted him sooner? Was he worried about the baby? It was his baby, too.

The child in her stirred. It felt different than it had the day before or even in the hours before the accident. But then, she could be imagining the whole thing. She could be completely out of her mind.

The swinging doors opened and her doctor walked in, as ever flanked by nurses, but this time followed also by Eli. She saw him before he saw her and their eyes met. She had a moment to just look at him and feel the same butterflies that she had felt the first time she had crashed into him at graduation. His eyes were as dark as ever, warm pools to fall into. She longed for him to pull her into his arms. She couldn't move enough to get up even if they would let her. She wanted him to gather her flush against him in a way she had never appreciated before. She swore to herself that she would let him have whatever he wanted. She just wanted to make it out of that operating room alive.

"Eli?" She called tentatively.

He was at her bedside in a second. Without hesitating he leaned down and kissed her deeply. She responded to his caresses eagerly, laughing and crying together. The music of the operating room followed them as she was wheeled into the surgery room. He never let go of her hands. His lips danced over her again and again, murmuring how much he loved her.

Essie sat up as much as she could, leaning into him. "Esmeralda, lie back down!" he cried in alarmed response.

She did so and pouted. "I…"

"I'm sorry. I just don't want you to exert yourself. I'm worried," Eli kissed her forehead. "I haven't seen you in so long, I… are you alright!"

"I'm in pain," Essie smiled weakly.

Eli paused, meeting her eyes and trying to decide what to say next. There were so many thoughts and feelings to be shared, questions to ask, and steps to make. There were not enough words. Eli thought about how close he was with Lena only hours ago. He remembered the brutal fight that Eli and Essie had shared. He remembered her coolly telling him to leave and sleep on the couch. He remembered angrily packing his bag and getting on a plane. Tabitha, his darling baby sister's, sharp words echoed in his mind. He winced, thinking that he had really repeated such hurtful things to his wife. His other half. His partner for life. Their eyes were still connected. Eli didn't know what to say. Should he apologize? He looked at her weepy, emerald-ice eyes and didn't even know if they could make it work. Did he come back because he was worried about her and it was just a habit? Did he come because he wanted to see his baby?

Essie, as he fell silent, drew back on the same spasm of fear that she had had earlier. Why was he back? How could they ever get back together after all that had happened? "Eli…?" She began, tentatively. "I…"

As she started to talk, the nurses took hold of her gurney and started to move it into place. A flood of celebrity-level narcotics swept through her body. Eli's grip tightened on her fingers and he trotted to keep up. "Esmeralda? Gem?"

She sighed deeply, her eyelids fluttering but not completely closing.

"What's wrong with her!" Eli demanded.

The nurse next to him shook her head laughing gently. "Don't worry. She's quite alright. And awake. Just adjusting to the new medications."

Eli looked down at the girl next to him. "Girl" was not an inaccurate description. She looked so young and vulnerable. He had to say something. He couldn't promise that everything was going to be okay. He couldn't promise that their marriage would work out perfectly. "I love you, Esmeralda," he murmured, kissing her cold cheek. It was the only promise that he could make and knew he could keep. "I love you. I will always love you."

She couldn't answer. She tried but words failed. Her little pink smile and returning squeeze to his fingers would have to do.

Dr. Laura Bird as well as Dr. Church met them in the operating room. "Okay people, let's get started," Dr. Bird clapped. The whole mood was quickly changed. It was more intense and focused. A blue curtain was set up shielding Eli and Essie from the view of the actual surgery.

"Don't peek," Dr. Church smirked. "It's about 60 minutes from here. And we're starting!"

Essie was in a haze of medications through the procedure, but Eli was wide awake and terrified. The nurse he had met in the hall (What was her name?) stood next to him, reassuringly speaking to him. As things progressed, she talked him through what was happening. Eli found that he was grossly fascinated by the medical side of the procedure. He thought that maybe if he hadn't had to become a lawyer and hadn't been too stubborn to consider other avenues of work, he might have become a doctor.

"There's the first incision!" she exclaimed.

Eli smiled at her childlike joy at the cutting open of his wife. It was almost comedic. He quickly looked back to check on how Essie was doing. She wouldn't think it was very funny if he was laughing with another woman about carving her. She still had her eyes half-closed, glancing off toward something no one else could see, a small smile on her little lips. He squeezed her hand reassuringly, and she responded quickly, if not weakly.

"That one will go through the skin and the abdominal wall, usually along the bikini line, meaning that it's low enough down on the pelvis that it would be covered up by underwear or a bikini bottom"

"Scars?" Eli asked. He knew that if she were awake, Essie would ask too. She would absolutely hate to have scars.

"Sometimes," the nurse shrugged. "Battle wounds?"

"I guess so," Eli glanced back at her again. He wouldn't care if she were scared. He would always think of this day in a horrid light yet a beautiful one. They were going to have a baby! It might be that the last 24 hours were awful, but they would make it. A little while passed. It seemed no more than a few minutes even as he watched her nervously. Then the nurse started excitedly.

"Don't look, but they're cutting the uterine wall!" The young nurse exclaimed. "Typically, a side-to-side (horizontal) cut is made, which ruptures the amniotic sac surrounding the baby. Once this protective membrane is ruptured, the baby is removed from the uterus, the umbilical cord is cut, and the placenta is removed."

Dr. Bird spoke up reassuringly from behind the curtain. "Okay, Esmeralda! On the home stretch now. You're going to feel a little tug and... Here we are! A baby girl! And blood pressure dropping back down already!" There was a weak little wail and Eli looked eagerly for the baby, but the room had suddenly turned into chaos.

The nurse was gone with a newly appeared detachment of other nurses and attendants, settling his daughter into a basket and wheeling her away.

"Eli?" Essie was awake and alert when he turned to tend to her. Her eyes were full of fear. "Eli, where are they taking her?"

He couldn't speak. They had said that the baby would be okay and that Essie would be, too! Everything was going to be fine. They had promised! So why were the flight attendants putting on gas masks?

The surgery wasn't finished yet. They still had to put the stitches into the cuts and clean everything from infection.

He grabbed one of the retreating nurses by the arm. "Where is she going!"

She shook him off. "To the nursery. She has to be in an incubator soon. She's very premature."

"Not that premature… only 6 weeks…"

"That's a lot. Please let go, Sir. We're the experts. We'll figure it out," she hurried out with the others.

Essie grabbed Eli's arm. "Elias, you have to go with her," she pleaded to look up at him in horror. "She's just a little baby! She has to have one of her parents with her! She's so little," Essie sobbed. "She must be so scared! You have to go! I can't go so you have to!"

Eli looked down at her. "But you—"

"I'll be fine! Please. Please go with her. I'll be fine!" Essie pushed him away and haltingly he followed after her.

In the hall, he was met by his family. His mom took one look at him and pulled him into a hug. His brothers were there, Lucas with his wife and the four youngest girls. Joanna hugged him fiercely. Tabitha was missing. His brothers squeezed his shoulders and Lucas's wife kissed his cheek while holding one hand knowingly over her own flat belly. Eli went to his mother and whispered to her, "They took our baby. I don't know where she is and I'm scared to find out."

"You've got to," Amy murmured.

"Mama, I can't," he shook his head. "She told me to go find her and be with the girl but what if that is her way of asking me to leave again!"

"Come on, Eli, you've got to go be with your baby."

"Will a baby fix everything, mom?" Eli said, hushed. "People say that having a baby will fix a marriage."

Amy looked thoughtful. "Maybe we should talk while we walk," she suggested wisely. Her other children pretended to look uninterested as she led her eldest away. She held his hand gently as if guiding a child. At this moment, the moment where some might say he was mostly a man, he was mostly a child, needing his mother to care for him.

"What was it like when I was born?" Eli asked suddenly.

"Believe it or not," Amy began, sparked with an idea of what she could tell him to keep his hopes up, "your daddy and I struggled with several of the same issues that you and Essie deal with. We were very young. I was only 21 and he was 25. I think that a huge part of the trouble in the church is that young people are getting married so young. You know, your brother Lucas and even Samuel. Johanna was 28, although you can imagine what some people said. That she would be a dried-up old spinster or that she would end up living in sin."

"Pastor James would never say such things, but our minister before him… you remember Petero—he preached weekly about the dangers of being alone. Don't get me wrong," She warned, "It's not good to be alone, but so many of the young people in the church get married so young and start having kids and then 53% of them end up divorced."

"The church doesn't provide them the tools to make it through the first year," Eli said, thinking back to the single couple's session he and Essie had attended before being married. It had been useless. He had gone into marriage thinking that it was forever and that love was the gushy feeling you got when you kissed someone you like. He had learned much just through living with Esmeralda for a year.

Love wasn't the warm wave or the soft tingly feeling you get when you spend time with someone you cared about. Love is doing the dishes when she is sick and tired at night even when you just want to sleep. Love is getting up to make him breakfast. It's waking up at three ante meridiem to massage her swollen ankles. It's staying up until past midnight to sew all new buttons on his shirt. Love is choosing each other over and over again, even when you wake up the morning after a huge fight with all the sharp things you said to each other looming in the air. Love is greeting her jovially anyway and love is making a pact to put the past in the past, learn from it, and move forward.

"Worse than that, the church doesn't talk about it. The only thing they say is that young people should marry young to keep themselves pure and have an accountable partner. The problem is that youth don't know why they are getting married! It just makes me crazy."

They were suddenly in front of the nursery. Through the glass walls, Eli could see rows upon rows of cradles, bassinets, and incubators.

"Children… on the other hand…" Amy continued softly. "Are an amplifier."

"What does that mean?"

"They amplify. If you have a beautiful God blessed relationship they'll strengthen and grow it. You and Joanna and Lucas were born in that era of our marriage. If you have some problems to work out… well… that was when Tabitha was born. A baby in hard times makes things harder. It also impacts the way the child grows up. That's why you and Jo and Lucas are responsible and kind and gentle and Tabby, well…"

"She's Tabby," Eli answered, habitually defending her.

"Right," Amy said with a ghost of a smile. She looked over Eli's shoulder and smiled for real. "I think you need to call your wife over right now and talk to her. You need to decide if you want to make this relationship work. And you can't do it only for the little one. You have to choose to work it out for yourselves and let your daughter be an asset, not a foundation."

From behind him, Essie's voice came clear. "I want it to work, Elias."

He turned and saw her, still strapped to her bed being wheeled down the hallway. The nurse left her parked by the window to the nursery and stepped away with Amy to give the couple some space.

"What did you say?" Eli asked, suddenly breathless and shy in her presence.

"I want us to work. I'm not giving up on you. I choose you," Essie repeated softly. "I love you."

"I love you too," Eli bent and kissed her, eyes closed against distraction.

"I love you so much," he took her hand and touched the two bands around her little fingers. He kissed her fourth finger mumbling, "With this ring, I thee wed. And I will be your husband and I will cherish and love you forever and ever.”

“With this ring, I thee wed,” Essie repeated, touching the gold band on his hand to her lips. “And I vow that I will love you and obey you and care for you until the end of forever and even after that.”

“And our baby will amplify our love.”

“Yes,” Essie agreed to lean up to kiss him. “By the way, Eli, you missed me getting 28 stitches in my belly. I’m going to have an amazing scar and a great story to tell after all of this.”

Eli looked at her in surprise. A month ago the idea of such a scar would have scared her into not wanting to have the baby. Yet here she was bragging about it. She had taken a step toward growing up while they had been apart.

“Careful now… mind her head,” the nurse said nervously as she placed the delicate baby into Eli’s arms.

Eli pulled away in annoyance. “I have eight younger siblings and 9 nieces and nephews. I *know* how to hold a baby!” The nurse stepped back doubtful but still letting him pick up the girl on his own and cradle her to his chest.

Eli stroked her soft downy head and admired the bluish-green of her eyes that the doctor promised would deepen into a forest green that would break the hearts of many little boys. Her hair, dark like his, was matted over her forehead. She had one perfect little curl dancing up off of her head.

Essie looked on, smiling all the way to her eyes as Eli bent and kissed their baby, blessing her in front of all his siblings as their first-born child. He placed the girl back in her mother’s arms and watched as his family cheered and filed past, blessing the little girl with everything they could think of. Joanna kissed Essie and offered a few words of motherly advice. Essie, glowing with pride, nodded and smiled as if she were listening, but really danced off through her own brain.

The little girl mewed and Eli was quick to scoop her back up. He knelt so his littlest sister could marvel at his daughter's tiny hands and fingers and toes and eyelashes. He was a father. He could hardly believe the miracle of God that this tiny bundle of beauty.

He stepped back to Essie's side and they held the girl together. "We never thought about names," he suddenly said, "We can't keep calling her 'the baby'."

"Esther," Essie suggested. "Look how beautiful she is."

"She is," Eli agreed. "But I want a name with a little more meaning to it."

"Mercy?" Essie proposed, looking up at Eli meaningfully.

"Joy?" he responded.

Picking up the little book of names by her bedside that had been a gift from her mother, Essie read out a few of her favorites. "Talitha, meaning young woman. Diana, luminous or perfect. Eva, meaning living… Areli! Child of God," she cried with triumph.

"Areli. Areli Eva Darcy."

"Ariel Eva Katelyn Darcy," she said firmly and then looked up at Eli. "If you don't mind? And if your sisters won't feel snubbed."

Again Eli was amazed by the change in her. The old Esmeralda that he knew would never have looked to him having already come up with something she liked. And she certainly wouldn't have asked if his sisters would be okay with it.

"Ariel Eva Katelyn Darcy," he agreed, kissing her gently on the mouth.

Four days later, Essie and Ariel were released from the hospital. Before they could go, the doctor and OB/GYN called the young couple into Dr. Church's office. They brought Ariel, all bundled up snug and warm in her soft green blankets. The doctors cooed over the baby and said all the right things, but their smiles were forced and Eli and Essie knew that it was all a show.

"Before we can let you go," Dr. Bird began, "we need to have a serious conversation. Between the medical conditions of both mama here and the little one, our earlier mentioned concern is very present and very real."

Essie stared down at the ground and when she looked up her eyes were full of tears. One slid down her pale cheek as she asked fearfully, "No more babies?"

Before the doctors answered, she held Ariel closer and kissed her. She leaned against Eli and he put his arm around her comfortingly.

"I'm sorry," Dr. Bird said gently.

Dr. Church looked perplexed. "This one is healthy and alive. Don't worry about future children. As first-time parents, I'm sure you'll find that one is enough."

Eli tapped down his irritation at the man as the obstetrician kicked the doctor's ankle with enough force that Eli had to hold back a wince. Elias was pleasantly and heartbreakingly surprised by Essie's tears. She hadn't even wanted one baby. Especially not this early in their marriage.

Yet here she was, crying at the news that she would never have another child.

As she had progressed through the pregnancy, the idea of having children and being a mother had grown on Essie. She had imagined having a son and teaching him how to tie a tie and help a lady with her coat. She had imagined having a son to take care of his younger sister. She had wanted to raise a perfect little gentleman who could cook for and defend his women all at once. She had considered the idea that they would have three or more little daughters only a few years apart. She would have sewn them matching dresses and marched them all off to church in a happy little procession. It was heartbreaking that all her tentative dreams would come crashing down around her just as they were starting to be built.

"Are you sure?" Eli asked as he held Essie close.

"The urgent nature of the surgery meant that the cuts were not meant to be cosmetic. There was a slip in the second cut in the uterine wall. We're sure. Even were it not for that cut, the risks attached to having another baby after what happened here with the Contra Coup and Preeclampsia would be too high. Don't risk it," Dr. Church answered.

Eli felt frustrated that part of the ensuing problem had been their error in the first place, but it was so quickly covered by a deep feeling of relief that he still had his beautiful, caring wife and baby girl, full of potential, that he wouldn't even dwell on it. "Thank you for everything that you have done," he said humbly. He took Essie's hand and kissed Ariel's head. "You saved my most precious treasures."

Chapter 9

The drive home was quiet. It was the first time that they had been really alone, just the three as a family, that they didn't know what to say. Eli and Essie had repeated their vows as soon as she had come out of surgery and they were reconciled to living out the rest of their lives together. They had reaffirmed love for each other, but it still felt like there was much more to say.

Pulling into the driveway, Eli loitered, not sure if he should turn off the engine and go in. He hadn't been in the house since he had left in such a tizzy. He imagined that the mess of his items spilled over the living room floor would still be there and anger would linger in every corner.

Essie didn't want to go into the house. She loved Eli and he loved her. They had talked about what forever meant and were determined that they would stick it out. But the last time she had been home she had been talking with Kate about divorcing him. Sitting beside her in the driver's seat, she could feel Eli hesitating as well.

There was no telling how long they would have sat there in silence, waiting for the other to speak first. Ariel broke the moment with a pitiful wail.

"Is she hungry?" Eli asked.

Essie looked back at the wide-eyed girl with her still wrinkled red face and indiscernible, ugly features. "Maybe," she unbuckled her seat belt, and walked around the vehicle, reaching for the car seat. Eli was already there, picking up their daughter tentatively.

"I've got it."

Their eyes met, and Essie had a sudden beautiful flash-forward of Elias as an amazing father. She imagined a chubby two-year-old throwing her arms around the father she adored and saying in her soft baby voice, "I love you, daddy." She saw him kneeling in front of four-year-old Ariel teaching her to tie her shoelaces. She saw him rubbing her back and holding her as she cried about some students being mean to her at 12. She envisioned Eli holding her in his arms and twirling her at age 16 in a daddy-daughter dance.

She looked back to the present and nodded, "Okay." Elias would be an amazing father. And Essie was glad. Her daughter would have all the things that Esmeralda hadn't had growing up.

Inside, the house was spotless. Everything had been tidied up and tucked away. It was the perfect balance of clean, yet homey. They found the note on the dining room table. It was from Kyra and Amy. They had cleaned everything up for them. They said congratulations and that they loved them both very much. The house smelled vaguely like cinnamon and vanilla. Essie found, in the investigation of the scent, that the baking jar, the one she had kept so religiously full, had been topped up with cookies.

Essie fed the baby and put her in bed without a problem. Then it was just her and Eli up. He was sitting in the living room on his phone, reading the news headlines of the day. She thought about doing some work on the needlepoint her mom had brought her while she was in the hospital but couldn't find the discipline to do cross-stitch at the moment.

She looked over at Eli, looking so comfortable on the couch. He looked like he belonged there. Like that was his house and his home. Essie didn't feel at home. She stood off to the side for an awkward moment. She had nothing to do other than just go to bed yet she felt she needed to do something to fix everything with her husband and feel like she belonged here again. There were so many things to say but no words. Eli looked up and saw her standing there, unsure of what to do. He put his arm up on the back of the chair in invitation. She went to him happily and snuggled under his arm.

There were no words exchanged. Essie knew that they would come eventually, but, for the time being, the home was there under his love.

The first night home without nurses to help her handle Ariel passed uneventfully. Essie woke up and fed her around midnight. The little girl fell asleep at her breast and Essie drifted off with her snuggled skin to skin. When Ariel roused needing to be changed and burped about half an hour later, Eli picked her up and changed her. Awakened by the muffled whimpers, Essie woke up as well and heard Eli mumbling and singing gently to her as they paced the hallway floor before Ariel slipped back into sleep and was tucked into her bassinet in the nursery. Eli returned to bed and sleepily reached for Essie. She turned to him happily, cuddled back to dreamland.

Essie had been afraid that she would sleep through Ariel's cries, but as it turned out, she slept quite poorly. Her senses were so tuned to listen for the baby that any motion in the room would send her wide awake. She took comfort in the fact that Eli had the same problem. In fact, every time that she was thrown into a state of panic-like consciousness, he was already up and soothed her back to sleep, running his hand over her hair and murmuring softly to her.

Essie woke up at 8 am having slept soundly for the last three hours. Elias had finally slid into a deep sleep and was snoring gently. Essie left him and his embrace, instinctively showering and heading for the kitchen. She wanted to make him breakfast.

She was right on time. About 45 minutes after she got up, Ariel cried out for attention and her breakfast. Essie heard Eli get up and pick up the baby, rocking her and cooing to her in the early morning air. She heard him pad through the bedroom and talk to her about the falling snow outside. He went back to the bedroom and settled Ariel in her playpen. When he came into the dining room, Essie was setting the table.

Eli took in the meal that Esmeralda had prepared. "Good morning," he said befittingly.

"Good morning," Essie answered timidly. There was a pause and then, "I made you pancakes."

Eli impulsively walked over and wrapped one arm around her waist. "They look delicious," he bent and kissed her. It was the kind of gesture he might have made casually, a month ago.

The familiarity and laid-back manner of the motion set Essie at ease and she leaned into the kiss. When they separated, Eli was grinning at her and Essie stared at him in confusion. "What?" She demanded.

"That's the first time that I've kissed you properly in too long," he answered.

Emboldened and missing him, Essie shook her head. "That wasn't properly. I'll show you," she entwined her arms loosely around his neck and stood on tiptoe as she pressed her lips against his sweetly. His arms came up around her waist and lower back, holding her ever so tightly against him and deepening the kiss. It turned passionate and went on for a long moment.

When she pulled away, flushed and a little bit shy, Essie was laughing. Eli chuckled and covered her mouth with his again. "Well done, wife. There is a thing or two that you could teach me. Show me again?" he teased.

"Of course, Mr. Darcy," she looked up at him from under her dark lashes and Eli felt his stomach flip. His wife. His beautiful, sweet, hard-as-emeralds bride.

"Look at her! Already two weeks old!" Kate cooed. She leaned over and kissed the baby's soft brown head.

Essie rocked her gently and smiled down at her. "I never expected to love being a mother so much," she giggled.

Ariel, starting to fall asleep in her mother's lap, opened her eyes again and let out a wail. Essie stood up and paced the room with her, singing quietly to her in time to the music playing upstairs.

"The best thing about having a baby, for sure," Kate remarked with a grin, "You have an excuse to leave a boring sermon."

Essie made a face at her. "I did not come down here to avoid church."

"M'kay, Ess." Kate laughed.

Essie walked back again across the church's basement. Ariel's eyelids fluttered closed over her big green eyes.

"She's so beautiful," Kate sighed. "Makes me want to have my own."

Essie looked down at the little girl in her doll-like dress and tiny toque. "She looked like a little alien," she giggled.

"Esmeralda!"

Essie giggled again. "But I love her so much. I wouldn't trade her for anyone."

Just as Ariel was falling asleep, the church service ended and people began trampling down the stairs. Essie thought with distaste the idea of everyone stomping downstairs and fawning over her almost sleeping baby. "Can we walk outside?"

Kate helped her with her coat and the little one's wraps. Outside in the brisk air, they were silent for a while. Essie sent a text message to Eli letting him know that she was alright and with Ariel and Kate.

Kate looked in surprise and defensively Essie responded, "What!"

"When did you start... submitting to him."

Essie made a face at her. "What on earth do you mean!"

"You never would have let him know where you were going and asking him if it was alright before... the incident."

Essie smiled faintly. "It's... nice."

"Nice?"

"Yes. Nice," she answered firmly. "Besides. I like him to let me know where he is and that he's okay so why shouldn't I do the same?"

"Because... I mean, there's no reason why you shouldn't. It's just not like you."

"Marriage changes a girl," Essie winked and went on walking, leaving her astonished friend to run to catch up.

Kate wasn't completely wrong. She had changed. She never would have done that before. But then, there were many things that she did now that she wouldn't have been caught dead doing before the incident. In the brief moments before Kate caught up and went on chattering, Essie reflected on her marriage.

She had gone into it so naive and with such childish thoughts and ideas. She hadn't had the slightest clue what it meant to be married. She hadn't known at all what it meant to be tied to someone forever and have them tied to her. Marriage was a beautiful thing that God had sanctified. She was blessed that she and Eli had been able to bounce back from the pit they had dug themselves into. She sent up a quick prayer for all the couples that she had seen and hadn't seen but knew existed that wouldn't make it through. 50% don't make it. The fact that she and Eli had was a pure miracle.

Essie remembered the last two weeks of their new marriage. It had taken some time to get to a sense of normality. She saw that Eli was being gentle with her and she knew she was acting differently in return. Some things slowly came back to them. He would casually wrap his arms around her tightly and rest his cheek on her head as if terrified that should he let go, she would be gone. She tried to tell him how much she loved him and spent as much time as she could cook for him and doing little things, ironing his shirts the night before, keeping the house tidy, having Ariel dressed prettily and happy for when he got home in the evenings.

She had looked into getting a job, but that didn't solve the immediate issue of their current financial situation. Then they had gotten the call from Greg. Eli and him had gotten the deal with the investors they had been meeting with. Essie got a call the same day that she had gotten a personal assistant position at Eli's old workplace. It was a job that Mrs. Grail had said she could bring Ariel with her to. Everything was looking up.

Kate caught up with her and, gasping for breath, exclaimed, "Wait, so that's it!"

"What do you mean now?"

"Everything is just peachy now? You're just going to go on as if none of the conflicts ever happened?" She shrieked.

Essie rolled her eyes. "It's all solved."

"I don't know much about marriage," Kate began, "but that's not how it works. Maybe you two should see a counselor together or something. Just to make sure that none of this comes back up."

Heading back toward the church with the sun setting and Ariel fast asleep in Essie's arms, it was easy to laugh at her friend. She could see Eli waiting for them at the front of the church. She ran into his arms, her heart full of love for him, just as it had been in their first months of marriage.

She didn't need to answer Kate as Elias drew her close and kissed her, then their daughter, his eyes warm with affection. They were going to be better than fine.

The End

Epilogue

Many years later

"Dinner!" Essie called. There was no response. She called again, "Eli! Dinner time!"

He answered with a faint, "I'm on my way up!" From the basement.

Essie nodded in satisfaction and adjusted a dish on the table to be more straight. She walked down the hall and knocked on the door to her daughter's room. "Ariel? Please wash your hands for dinner. Daddy will be up soon and I don't want to keep him late. You know his friend Greg wants to get this project done soon."

About halfway through her monologue, Essie realized she'd been talking to herself. "Ariel!" she exclaimed and shook her daughter's shoulder.

Ariel looked up from the piano and then dismissively looked back down. Impatient, Essie shook her again. "Ariel! Now," She ordered.

The little girl shrugged and rolled her eyes in a way altogether too teenager-y for an eight-year-old. "Don't roll your eyes at me," Essie snapped.

"Mama," Ariel whined.

"Go to the table!" Essie picked her up off of the piano bench and set her on her feet. Ariel whined and mumbled to herself as she slinked to the bathroom and then to the dining room. Essie followed along behind, picking up the hand towel Ariel left trailing on the floor without a word. This was not the angelic girl she had hoped for. She was sullen and rude—except to her father.

Ariel slouched at the table, glaring at the meal her mother had labored over. Essie took her seat with a serene smile for her girl and then yelled impatiently, "Mr. Darcy!"

"I'm coming! Just one more second!" he called back.

Essie stood with a hand on one hip. "Ariel, don't move," she commanded and marched down the stairs. Eli was lying back in his chair, a blueprint held up to his nose. Essie pulled it back and exclaimed. "Dinner? And where are your glasses! You shouldn't have to hold it so close to your face!"

Eli leaned up to kiss her. "I don't need the glasses. I'm 40, not elderly," he joked.

Essie pulled away from him with a frown. "Elias, it's dinner time. Could you please come upstairs? And have a chat with your daughter? She's grating on my very last nerve."

"Oh, she's *my* daughter now," he teased. His face and tone turned sober. "Essie, we've made it this far—"

"Dinner is getting cold," she said icily.

Elias kissed her fingertips fondly and stood up. "Okay, gem."

Essie whirled around and started to head toward the stairs when she heard the piano in the living room playing. With an exclamation of frustration, she flew up the stairs and grabbed Ariel's wrist before the girl can touch another note. "I told you to stay at the table!" she scolded.

"You and daddy were talking for so long," Ariel complained. She trotted to keep up as her mother drags her back to the table. She pouted, "It's not my fault! I have to learn that piece for my next lesson. Auntie Tabitha says…"

"I don't care what your aunt says!" Essie cried.

Ariel sank into her seat with a glare and a stuck-out lower lip. "You don't have to be so mad at me."

"I wouldn't if you would do what you were told!" Essie fired back. "Elias!"

Eli's steps could finally be heard coming closer. He set his newspaper on the table and took his seat. "Ariel, please listen to your mom," he began. The meaning was taken out of his words; by the way, he encouraged Ariel to jump out of her seat to embrace him. Her eyes shining with a pretty smile, she beamed up at her daddy as they chatted about their days and the new piano piece Ariel was learning.

As Essie dished out the meal she had prepared, she was struck with the same left-out feeling she always got when Ariel and her father talk. They were so close. They bonded immediately, but Essie had never felt that way for the girl. She just… annoyed her so much!

Essie set the plates down hard and, on one, steamed vegetables sprayed in all directions across the table. They all fell silent.

"Why don't you bless the food, Gem," Eli said to Essie with a warning glance.

Essie obliged but chafed at being told what to do by Eli in front of their snickering brat of a child. She mumbled a prayer and then picked up her fork.

Ariel picked at her food. "Daddy, may I be excused?" She asked after only a few minutes.

"Is something wrong with your plate?" Essie cut in.

Ariel shot her a side glance and mutters, "I didn't ask you."

Essie raised her eyebrows at Eli as if to say, 'see! I told you!'. "You're going to sit there until it's all done and don't talk back to me, young lady!" she snapped.

Ariel sank lower in her seat and pouted.

"Sit up, Ariel," Elias said quietly. "And don't speak to your mother that way. You can go after you eat 5 more bites."

"And can I have dessert?" Ariel pushed.

"No!" Essie cut her off.

"We'll see," Elias said at the same time. There was a pregnant moment of silence before Essie got up and threw her napkin on her plate. Her chair fell backward with a screech.

"Where are you going?" Elias asked, concerned.

"Away," Essie glared and clipped down the hall, grabbing her coat and her purse. Before she slammed the door, she heard Ariel asked again, "Can I have ice cream?" And Eli's murmured 'hush.'

Essie came back to the house two hours later. Only one light was on as she opened the door. Eli was waiting for her at the top of the stairs. She stared at the ground.

"Oh, Esmeralda," he said.

Essie felt irritation once again. His tone was disapproving. She didn't move. "Where were you?"

"I was out," Essie answered shortly.

"You ignored all of my calls," Eli scolded. "I was worried about you," Eli gestured for her to come upstairs, ending their standoff.

Essie walked into the dining room and saw that Eli had done the dinner dishes. Two empty ice cream bowls sat on the table with spoons and the monopoly board. Half a bowl of popcorn was there too. Essie took a seat in the living room and asked, "Did she go to bed alright?"

"Yes," Elias responded. He hesitated, looking for other words.

"Good," Essie nodded. There was a pause.

Elias took a seat on the couch and put an arm around Esmeralda. She froze, not leaning into him.

"Did she finish her dinner?" Essie looked straight at him.

Eli looked away. "Esmeralda…"

"You always do that, Eli!"

"Do what?"

"Contradict me in front of her! Don't make me the bad guy! It's no wonder you and her are so close. You basically tell her that my word means nothing since if I say no, she can always run to you and you'll give it to her," Essie scooted away from him to look accusatorily at him.

"I don't do that," Eli frowned.

"Oh, really? The piano lessons with *your sister*, the new clothes once a month and pizza lunches once a week. The cell phone!" Essie folded her arms.

Eli raised his voice. "Get off your high horse! You're so hard on her! Is it wrong for me to want to soften things a little!"

"It is when you make me look bad when doing it!" Essie screamed.

Little feet padded down the hallway and a soft face with two brown braids framing it. "Daddy? Mama?"

Essie sighed. "Come here, Ariel."

For once in her sleepy fear, Ariel went to her mother instead of her father. "What's going on?" she asked.

Essie and Eli didn't look at each other. Ariel looked even more frightened. "Are you getting a divorce?" she started crying. "Jason told me that his parents got a divorce when they were yelling at each other."

Now Eli did look at Essie. In surprise. He hadn't known that Ariel knew what had happened to Joanna and her husband. The whole family was caught off guard and had tried to protect the kids from it.

"No, we're not getting divorced," Eli said light-heartedly. He picked Ariel up and went down the hall to tuck her back into bed. From the living room, Essie could hear their quiet voices and Ariel's laugh.

Eli came back and pulled her against him. Essie went willingly. In the almost nine years since they were married, he hadn't gotten any less handsome. In fact, other than Ariel, everything had gone according to Essie's plan. She wished that she had gotten along better with Ariel from a young age. When it became clear that Ariel would always prefer her daddy, Essie wished that she could have had another baby to love. They just couldn't afford to adopt, and one dangerously violent miscarriage had scared them off. Essie had never realized how much children had played into her larger plan of life.

Eli kissed her forehead, wondering what she was thinking. "Esmeralda…" He breathed, "What's going on with us."

"I don't know," Essie sighed, blinking back tears.

"I think… do you think… we should maybe… go back to counseling?" Eli suggested tentatively.

"No," Essie snapped. "We tried that, remember. For the first year after Ariel was born. It was a disaster. I won't go back."

"Gem, we have to do something," Eli countered.

"That woman was crazy! She kept blaming me for everything and saying that it was because of my mom's distance and relationship problems!" Essie's pitch started to rise again, and Eli made a meaningful face.

"We can find a different couples counselor," Eli promised.

Essie sighed, "I don't know. I didn't like it."

"Tell me this, do you want our relationship to work out?" Eli asked.

"Yes," Essie answered quickly.

"Then we have to do something different," Eli said.

"We can do it?" She looked to him for reassurance.

"Of course, we can."

"You don't think we're making too big of a deal out of nothing, right? Maybe this will solve itself," Essie suggested.

"Esmeralda, you know that's not true," Eli shook his head.

They were quiet for another long moment. Eli held her close to him and then kissed her gently.

“So, counseling?” Essie repeated, snuggling against his chest.

“Yeah,” he kissed her again.

“And we’ll live happily ever after. The end,” Essie said.

Eli shook his head. “Not the end. The beginning.”

Essie wrinkled her nose. “Corny.”

“You love me anyway,” Eli winked.

“I do love you,” Essie relaxed.

“Good. Cause I love you too,” Eli winked.

www.ingramcontent.com/pod-product-compliance
Lightning Source LLC
Chambersburg PA
CBHW071617030726
47598CB00001B/319